THE MISADVENTURES OF MISS ADELAIDE

MAGGIE DALLEN

CHAPTER 1

Miss Adelaide Hopewell was no more comfortable with the hustle and bustle of the Earl of Tolston's giant kitchen now than she had been the day she arrived nearly a fortnight earlier.

"Out of the way, girl," the head cook said as she brushed past.

"Pardon me," Addie murmured.

She moved quickly through the workspace which was teeming with servants as the household worked to prepare the townhouse for the arrival of the Earl himself. He was expected two days hence after being abroad these last few months, from what Addie could gather.

Not that anyone told her much. She was merely a maid these days, and maids, she'd soon realized, were rarely privy to much pertinent information regarding the lords and ladies of the house.

Or at least, *new* maids were not privy. Perhaps once she'd been there for more than a fortnight she might start learning about this Earl other than the whispers and snippets she overheard.

What she heard had not made him seem terribly appealing. Words such as *kind, honorable,* and *noble* had never been used. More like *firm, demanding,* and *cynical.* She'd once heard one of the stablemen refer to him as grim.

Grim.

That hardly evoked a pleasant image. Was it any wonder she was dreading his arrival? Of course, his impending arrival was the only reason she'd been hired on in the first place. The housekeeper had reckoned that with the Earl in London for the season, they'd require more maids—more maids who might be able to double as ladies' maids, in particular.

She wouldn't be surprised if the housekeeper anticipated many female guests. It did not take household gossip for her to know that the *ton* was expecting the Earl of Tolston to court and marry in the near future.

Addie made her way through the seemingly endless maze of hallways in this grand old house. She'd been raised in a lovely estate up north, and while her father, the Baron of Wrencliff, had indeed taken a good deal of pride in their family home, their estate could not hold a candle to the opulence and elegance of the Earl's residence.

The memory of her home brought with it a familiar pang that she staunchly ignored. Wallowing never did anyone any good, that was what her father used to say. She'd made her decisions, and now it was time to embrace them. She reached the staircase, freshly folded linens in one hand as she looked up at the high ceilings, fighting a case of vertigo as her gaze followed the spiral staircase up and up and up.

Was it possible a home could be too large? She suspected so. Particularly this one with its single occupant who was rarely in residence.

Once again, a vision rose up, this time unexpected so it nearly swept her off her feet. A memory, to be precise. The morning after her little brother was born—nearly two years ago now. She and her father had celebrated with pastries and tea, toasting one another in the pale glow of dawn as baby Reginald cried his little lungs out with a nursemaid while her mother slept.

She supposed now that morning was the last truly happy memory of her home. Shortly after that, her idyllic life in the country had turned to a nightmare. First her mother died of complications from the birth, and then not long after that, her father had followed with a sickness that moved fast and fierce, turning her healthy and hale Papa to a withered shell of himself in what felt like a heartbeat.

And then he too was gone, and Addie had supposed—rather naively, it turned out—that his death was the last of her turmoil.

But no. She'd soon discovered her hardships were only just beginning.

Her stomach churned, but whether it was from the memories or her hunger, she could not quite say. Maybe it was just exhaustion that made her feel so ill.

She took a deep steadying breath as she prepared herself for another hike up this magnificent staircase. Perhaps it was the fact that her position had her racing up and down the stairs countless times a day, but Addie was certain this house was entirely too big.

And to think, his estate in the country was said to be even more grand. She could hardly imagine.

She walked up three steps and paused with one hand on the bannister. She closed her eyes. Taking a deep breath, she waited patiently for this wave of dizziness to pass.

She would *not* faint. Maids did not swoon, everyone knew that.

Gently bred young ladies from the north might, but that was not she. Not any longer.

She pressed her eyes shut tightly as the world seemed to

3

spin around her. Deep breaths. One. And then another. This was the way to get through the falling sensation.

She'd survive it. She always did.

"What are you doing dallying here on the steps?" The housekeeper's brisk tone had her eyes snapping open once more.

"Sorry, Mrs. Harper."

The housekeeper grunted in response, her breath coming in loud huffs as she hitched up her skirts and hurried up the steps at a rate that was rather alarming considering her large size and elderly age. "Don't just stand there, Addie. Get back to work."

"Yes, ma'am." She followed the older woman, attempting to ignore the way the stairs seemed to shift and dip beneath her feet, and the way the walls around her did not appear to be as solid as one might hope.

Deep breaths. One and then another. That was the way.

Mrs. Harper's voice seemed to be coming to her through a tunnel. "They've sent word ahead that one of the party has suffered an injury," she said. "I've sent Will to fetch the doctor, he should be here shortly..."

Addie nodded, though the words seemed to be fighting their way through a fog. She squinted at Mrs. Harper's backside as the edges of her vision grew blurry and then dark. She stopped focusing on her breathing to focus on the steps. One step, two steps, three steps—

Floor.

She hit the second-floor landing with a thud and a jolt of nausea and that was the last thing she knew before blackness overtook her vision and she felt herself pulled under into unconsciousness.

When she woke she was on her back, still on the floor.

No, that wasn't quite right. There was something hard against her back, propping her up. When she blinked her eyes open, she found herself staring into the warmest, darkest pair of eyes she'd ever seen.

She was so dazzled by their warmth that she forgot she was supposed to think.

Or breathe.

Or move.

Perhaps she was not quite back in her right mind because she felt as though she might be dreaming. If she were, she hoped it would not end. She wouldn't mind lying here forever, gazing up dreamily into those warm brown eyes.

Unfortunately, Mrs. Harper interrupted the moment. "Addie. *Addie*, dear, are you all right?" The housekeeper's voice beside her had her tearing her eyes away long enough to see the older woman hovering over her, her wrinkled brow furrowed in concern.

Addie wanted to tell her yes, she was fine, but her voice wouldn't seem to work. Her throat was closing in, and her mouth went dry.

Reality was starting to creep in, and she was remembering it all.

Everything.

She was remembering too much all at once.

All her careful maneuvers to compartmentalize and focus on one problem at a time went out the window as her brain rushed to fill in every gaping hole at once.

She was a maid. She was friendless. She had no family, except for a little brother who was utterly dependent on her and her alone.

Her eyes widened with horror, not merely at her situation but at the fact that tears were beginning to sting the back of her eyes.

She *never* cried.

Well, not unless she was grieving. But she refused to wallow over her situation.

She couldn't afford to lose control, not now when Reggie needed her to be strong.

She found herself looking up into those eyes again, clinging to the connection like an anchor, seeking out that warmth. That little bit of human kindness.

He was handsome. Strikingly so. A lock of dark hair fell over his forehead, and lovely lush lips softened what was otherwise a stern set of features. But she didn't mind the sternness, nor the way his brows were a rather harsh slant as he frowned down at her. Because his eyes gave him away, what with all that warmth he could not hide.

She could gaze up at him for ages.

"What is wrong with her?" Mrs. Harper asked the gentleman who was holding her in his laps.

The doctor. Of course. Mrs. Harper had sent for a doctor.

This stranger must be the doctor who'd been sent for. Sure enough, his tone was all assured confidence as he rattled off instructions to Mrs. Harper. "Go fetch her some water, a cool cloth..." His eyes roamed over her face like he was taking a tally of her every freckle. "And some food, I think. She is far too pale."

Mrs. Harper hurried off, and Addie found herself alone. With a strange man.

And she found that she could not quite muster any embarrassment. She was too busy trying to shove her problems back in the pigeonholed recesses of her mind where they belonged. She could stew and worry to her heart's content later when she was asleep in her bed in the servants' quarters.

"Have they been working you so very hard?" The gentleman's voice was little more than a murmur. Low and soft, she quite liked listening to him.

He shifted, and she realized then that his arms were wrapped around her as she lay nestled on his lap. It was wildly inappropriate but also...rather lovely. For the first time in what felt like forever, she felt safe and coddled and protected.

It could not last, of course. Even in her addled state, she knew that. And yet, she could not quite bring herself to stir.

Even if she wanted to, she was not quite certain she was able. Her limbs felt like they were being held down with chains, and her head had that fuzzy feeling going on, along with a dull, persistent ache.

She must have winced as she took note of the headache, which was growing fast because the doctor shifted again to rest a hand against her forehead. "Some water and food should help. I don't feel any bumps, and it doesn't appear that anything is broken."

She gave her head a slight shake. No. Nothing broken... just her heart, and her dreams, and her future.

But no bones, and she supposed that was what he'd meant.

His hand on her forehead moved so he was smoothing her hair back. "Tell me, little one, have they been treating you so terribly here? You look as though you're starving and exhausted."

She blinked up at him. She supposed she *was* starving, but not because they did not feed her. Only because her food was needed by another. And she was indeed tired, but that was because her nights were sleepless with worry.

"They do not treat me poorly." It was the first time she'd spoken since waking, and she was horrified by how breathy she sounded.

How *weak*.

Concern tinged his eyes, making their dark shade even darker. From this angle it was difficult to say whether they were dark brown, gray, or just black as midnight. She almost asked him, but then he did the unthinkable. He moved his gaze and his hands to her body.

She tensed, but even as she went rigid at a stranger's touch, she knew that she had nothing to fear. He was a doctor, after all, and his touch spoke to his profession. His hands roamed over her briskly like he was straightening his cravat or tugging at his cuffs. The touch was impersonal as he ran a hand down her arms, her sides. "Does anything hurt?" His frown made her want to smile, oddly enough. It had been a long time since someone had been so concerned about her welfare. "There's a chance you've bruised a rib, or done some other damage that we cannot see."

He was murmuring again, and the sound of his voice had her closing her eyes as though he were singing a lullaby and not muttering to himself about her health.

"Open your eyes, little one." His thumb brushed her cheek, and she had to work to flutter her eyes open.

"Little one." She repeated the endearment like a dolt, rolling the words on her tongue like he'd spoken a foreign language. Indeed, it was only surprise that had her repeating it, because it was something one might say to a child. At nineteen she was hardly a child, though she supposed she looked younger than her years thanks to wideset eyes and a narrow chin. Her light brown hair was pulled back in a simple knot, and she imagined how she must look to him in this serviceable, yet decidedly ugly frock.

She shut her eyes tightly once more, this time out of embarrassment at her current state. She was a servant. She should not be lying here, lounging about when there was work to be done. She made a valiant effort to stir, and it was humiliation all over again when he restrained her with the gentlest touch to her shoulder. "Easy now, child."

"I am not a child," she managed. But again—too breathy. Too weak.

She sounded like... Well, she sounded like a *child*.

This would not do.

"Please, sir, allow me to sit upright," she said.

One of his brows hitched up ever so slightly. "I'd rather not have you fainting again, Miss..."

She opened her mouth to say Hopewell but caught herself just in time. This episode had so thoroughly rattled her brain that her mind when blank when she tried to recall her new, fictitious name. She stared at him with wide, panicked eyes for a moment before blurting out her first name. "Adelaide."

Something like amusement flickered in those captivating eyes as he considered her. "Miss Adelaide...what?" He prompted her for her surname, and she swallowed hard.

"Just Miss Adelaide."

There was definitely a glint of laughter in his eyes now, and more than a hint of curiosity as he glanced meaningfully from her to the spot where Mrs. Harper had disappeared. "I see," he said slowly. "So you are Miss Addie Adelaide?"

She pressed her lips together in annoyance with herself for getting flustered. With *him* for seeing through her stupid lies. And, oddly enough, with Mrs. Harper for so loudly shouting at her by the informal nickname she used below stairs, Addie.

Tillman! Of course, *now* the fictitious surname came to her —too little too late. "I, uh...that is, you see..." She found herself babbling incoherently as she scrambled to think of an explanation, something to excuse her fainting and a reason for why she was acting like an addle-brained ninny—but she was cut short when he reached for her hand.

She couldn't breathe let alone speak as he held her bare hand in his, like it was the most natural thing in the world.

Then again, maybe for a doctor it was.

His brow furrowed in concentration as he studied her palm and then her fingers, his own hand sliding over hers as if he were studying some new specimen. Her heart fluttered wildly in her chest at the gentle touch that belied his intense scrutiny.

"What are you—" Her protest was cut short when his eyes shot up to meet hers.

She gasped at what she saw there. Gone was the warmth, the tenderness. Instead those dark eyes blazed with accusation. "You are not a servant."

She blinked rapidly in surprise before understanding dawned. Her hands were soft and creamy white—the hands of a lady, minus the newfound burns and scratches that were a brilliant red against her pale skin. She jerked her hand out of his grasp, scrambling to sit upright despite the sick feeling that weighed on her.

He did not try to stop her, but his fierce gaze followed her every movement as she scrambled backwards. "Who are you?" he asked.

She glared at him. Anger was so much nicer than fear. Or worry. Or panic. She clung to that anger stubbornly. "I already told you, sir—"

"Ah yes," he said, his voice a sarcastic drawl. "Miss Addie Adelaide, how could I forget?"

She clamped her mouth shut and settled for the cold stare that her guardian had been so fond of employing with the servants.

To her annoyance, the stare only seemed to amuse him further. He was outright smirking at her, the irksome man. What sort of doctor smirked at his patient like that?

The thought had her looking around for Mrs. Harper. Surely she'd be back soon, and Addie could make her escape. Or the doctor would tell the housekeeper of his suspicions and...oh dear, what then? Panic struck her like a blow to the head. Her breathing grew shallow as she fought against this dreadful drowning sensation.

It ought to feel familiar by now, but it didn't. Panic and

fear were just as overwhelming and crippling now as they were three weeks ago when she'd snatched Reggie from the nursery and run away from home.

"Be easy, child." The doctor's voice was once more low, gentle, and kind. "No one will hurt you here. I only mean to help."

Help. *Ha!* No one could help her, and certainly not this man.

"I am not a child," she said with as much dignity as she could muster.

Which wasn't all that much, really, considering she was being strangled by a fit of fear.

Fear that she'd have to flee again, that she'd be forced to start all over again, and this time with even less options because she could not ask her second-cousin Emmaline to lie and give her a false reference again.

Once had already been too great a favor.

Besides, she could not risk showing up at her cousin's house and being recognized by Emmaline's parents. They would have questions. Too many questions.

Worse, they might try to send her and Reggie back to Duncan, her father's cousin and their legal guardian.

It was something of a miracle that no one yet knew she and Reggie were gone. At least, she assumed she would have seen her name in the newspaper by now if Duncan wanted it known that she'd gone missing. But she'd seen no news of her and Reggie's disappearance and had heard no gossip about a runaway lady and her infant brother.

When she was feeling optimistic, she liked to believe that maybe Duncan was happy to let them be. Without Reggie in the picture, he could have it all. The money, the title, the land. That was what he wanted, after all.

But then again—so long as Reggie lived, he posed a threat to Duncan's selfish desires.

Addie swallowed thickly now, trying to beat the fear back into submission. It was pointless to sit here and wonder what Duncan might say or do. The man was unhinged. Bizarrely kind one moment and then overset by rage the next... It was useless to try and predict his next move.

As long as he stayed silent about her disappearance, she'd choose to believe that Duncan had let them go without a fuss. For, if he spoke up about them leaving, he would have questions to answer, wouldn't he? And there was no way he could wish the truth to be known.

After all, Duncan could not want it to be known that he'd scared her off by threatening to kill her baby brother, now would he?

No. Certainly not.

She took a deep calming breath, ignoring the curious stare that was fixed on her.

It was best to focus on the most obvious conclusion. Duncan would wish to declare them deceased as quickly as he could and thank his lucky stars that he'd managed to get rid of Reggie—the rightful heir to whom the estate was entailed —out of the picture with little muss or fuss.

"I could help you, you know." His voice was so close she started. He'd shifted so he was leaning over her, holding out a hand as if to help her to her feet. Something about the gesture—so civil and kind. So thoughtful and so unexpected...

She eyed it warily, and then, for the first time in a long time...she lost the battle with tears.

It happened so quickly she stunned herself with the sudden waterworks. She must have stunned him as well, but it was difficult to say, what with all the tears clouding her vision. She sniffled wildly and swiped at her eyes, hoping to end this horrific outburst.

She *never* cried.

And certainly not over strange handsome doctors who offer their assistance.

She felt a handkerchief being pressed into her hand and hiccupped a thank you.

It was just that it had been so long since someone had been on her side, since someone had offered her help or spoken to her so gently.

Like she was someone to be cherished and heard and...and *believed*.

"I'm sorry," she whispered.

A warm, strong hand cupped her cheek, and with a touch so gentle it nearly made her cry all over again, he wiped away the last of her tears. "You are not a servant," he said again, this time not as an accusation but as a statement of fact.

She shook her head. No. She wasn't. Or...she hadn't been until recently, which she supposed was what he'd meant.

"Did you run away, or were you turned out?" Again with the quiet question, like he was the only other person in the world and no one else existed and like her answer did not change things.

"I ran." Oh, how she hated this wobbly, thin voice. Her jaw worked as she tried to subdue another wave of tears. She tilted her chin up so she was facing him head on. "Please don't tell Mrs. Harper."

It was a plea. She was begging, there was no doubt about it. But what did she care? She had little pride to cling to, and whatever was left was worth tossing away if it meant she could keep providing for Reggie's care.

He was eyeing her oddly. "You do not wish for Mrs. Harper to know?"

She shook her head. "She'll tell Lord Tolston, and they will toss me out and—" She reached for his hands without thinking. Gripping them with all her might, she was distantly aware of what a scene she must be making, now on her knees as he hovered over her. "Please do not tell. I promise you I meant no harm and I will learn to be a good servant, and—"

"Ah, here we are!" Mrs. Harper's voice carried up to them from the flight of stairs below. "My apologies for the delay, but the doctor arrived while I was fetching some bread."

The words took a moment to register, and as they did, she maintained eye contact with the gentleman with the warm dark eyes and the low kind voice.

"Looks like I arrived in the nick of time." A jovial male voice followed Mrs. Harper up the staircase. "Where is my patient?"

The doctor.

Addie blinked up at this gentleman whose expression was now entirely unreadable. But if that man coming up the stairs was the doctor, then who—

"Addie will be in good hands now, my lord," Mrs. Harper said briskly as she joined them on the landing. "You just leave her to us."

My lord.

She'd called him *my lord.*

Her breath caught in her throat, and the sound that came out of her mouth could only be described as a squeak of alarm.

She had just revealed her secret to the Earl of Tolston.

Her employer.

Her heart plummeted as she let Mrs. Harper help her to her feet.

It was over. Her one chance to start over, and now she was back where she was in the beginning.

On the run.

CHAPTER 2

Of all the ways Alec Finley, The Earl of Tolston, had imagined his homecoming to London, finding a lady splayed out on the floor unconscious in his house had not been one of them.

"Is it not too early for a drink?" Alec's cousin Gregory was sprawled out on a leather chair in the corner of his study, watching Alec pour the amber liquid into a glass. Gregory's injured leg was propped up in front of him on an ottoman.

"Do you need me to bring the doctor in here for that?" Alec asked, gesturing toward the leg.

Gregory waved him aside. "My sprained ankle is nothing compared to a lady in distress."

Alec frowned down into his drink. A lady. That was exactly what Miss Addie Adelaide was. She was gently bred, that much was certain. He'd suspected something was different about her from the start. From the moment she'd opened her eyes and met his gaze head-on, not differing or wavering or dipping her chin out of courtesy.

Then she'd spoken in that enchanting voice of hers, and

he'd heard it. The soft round vowels, the perfect elocution. It was the voice of a well-bred young lady, not a scullery maid.

It was her hands that had confirmed it for him. No one who worked for a living had hands so soft and pale. Her hands had been untouched up until very recently, he'd have bet his life on it.

So, what was a gently bred lady doing working as a maid in his London home?

"Ah, there's my patient." The portly doctor entered with a grin as he took in the sight of Gregory. "Heard you got thrown off a horse." He arched his brows. "And here I thought you were a good horseman."

Gregory winced. "I *am* a good horseman. Just...not in the middle of the night after a few rounds at the pub."

Alec gave his younger cousin a wan smile. "I told you we should have ridden straight through on that last leg of the journey."

"Yes, yes, you're very wise." Gregory's sarcasm was lost on no one. Alec didn't mind since sarcasm was one of the few things he had in common with his smiling, optimistic cousin.

The purpose of Gregory's stay was to find himself a bride. To imagine, Gregory was actually looking forward to settling down with a wife and children.

Alec intended choose a wife, as well, but he didn't pretend to be happy about it. There was no denying the fact that time was passing him by, however. He was not getting any younger, and he knew his duties well. Unlike some of his friends, he'd never thought to shirk his obligations to his title, only...put them off for a while.

But this was the season when he finally paid the piper and set aside his bachelor ways. Make no doubt about it. He *would* choose a wife.

He threw back the contents of his glass in one large gulp.

He'd do it. But he wouldn't be happy about it. It was just one more duty to add to the list of obligations that consumed his life. Not that he was complaining. He had a good life, he knew that he did. If he were a bit cynical, there was reason for it. He supposed that was the downside of having the world at one's fingertips. When one experienced every pleasure and still did not know true happiness, some pessimism was to be expected.

But he knew that he was a lucky man—and moments like the one he'd just had were a startlingly clear reminder of his good fortune.

He set the glass down with a thud at the memory of that look in her eyes.

Panic, plain and simple.

But why? And more importantly, why did he have this overwhelming urge to come to her aid?

Never in his life had he suffered from a knight-in-shining-armor complex. He'd had friends who'd fallen into that trap. Fools, every one of them. But never him. He understood he had an obligation to those less fortunate, but there were charities for that sort of thing.

He supposed, now that he thought about it, he'd never before been faced with a damsel in distress.

The voices of Gregory and the doctor were a vague background noise as he pondered that. He'd never had to come to anyone's aid before, not really. His friends were just as fortunate as he, if not more so, and he had little family left to speak of, aside from Gregory.

Even so, the surge of protectiveness—possibly even possessiveness— when he'd seen her fear...It had been disturbing, to say the least.

One thing was clear. The girl needed help.

But more than that, he needed her out of this house as soon as possible.

When the doctor was heading out, Alec called to him. "Send Mrs. Harper in, would you?"

"Of course."

A moment later she was there—his tried and true housekeeper who'd been with him for more years than he could count. "Did she have a reference?"

He no longer bothered with niceties with Mrs. Harper. He had no inclination toward subtlety, and Mrs. Harper had no time for idle chatter. The woman was forever on the move.

She straightened with a sniff. "Of course, my lord. Miss Tillman had a glowing reference from one of the young ladies of Lord Havershams' household."

He exchanged a look with the ever-curious Gregory. The Havershams were a good family, from what he knew of them. Decent people in good standing. Surely not the type to lie to his housekeeper. What was more—they were not the sort one *accused* of lying to one's housekeeper.

Mrs. Harper folded her hands in front of her. "My lord, if Miss Tillman has offended you in any way—"

"No, no, of course not," he said. "I am merely concerned, that is all. No member of my staff should be fainting on the staircase due to lack of food or sleep."

She dipped her chin with a huff. "I can assure you, sir, that is not the case. Everyone receives the same allotment of food and an adequate amount of time for sleep—"

He held up a hand to stop her. "I have no doubt that you take excellent care of my staff, Mrs. Harper. But you must admit that what happened today was unusual."

She pressed her lips together in response like she was irritated by the whole matter. He could not blame her; he was irritated as well.

One hour in London and he was already dealing with issues within his own household.

Less than a day, and he'd somehow found himself ensnared in some other family's drama.

He hated how much his curiosity ate at him, how badly he wanted to learn the young lady's secrets, but above and beyond all that, he knew he had to find a solution. And quick.

If she were indeed a ruined lady hiding in his household, that could only lead to gossip and speculation if it were discovered. It wasn't his own reputation he cared about, but hers. What she was *doing* living here in an unwed gentleman's home with no chaperone?

There was no going back from this.

He might not understand what had scared the girl, but he knew better than to allow an unwed gently bred young lady to reside within his home. If she changed her mind and wanted back into society, or if her family came looking for her...his home was the last place she ought to be found.

He had a startlingly vivid mental image of her face tipped up toward his, of the way she felt in his arms, of the delectable pink lips that had looked so sweet and yet revealed so little. The wide-set, innocent eyes that seemed to beg him for help.

His heart did an odd maneuver in his chest.

No, Miss Tillman—if that was indeed her real name— could only cause trouble in his household. For herself, for his staff...and for his own peace of mind.

"I'd like a word with her," he said.

Gregory interjected. "Oh Alec, leave the poor girl alone. She's likely already embarrassed enough, what with assuming you to be the doctor." He laughed at the mere idea, and Alec had to hide a wince as Mrs. Harper's eyes widened in horror.

"She took you to be..." She clapped her hands together in distress. "Oh, dear heavens."

"It's quite all right, Mrs. Harper." He shot Gregory a chastening look that he hoped clearly expressed the sentiment, '*I told you that in confidence, you ungrateful cur.*'

Gregory's smile never faded. He'd found the misunderstanding humorous in the extreme, whereas Alec merely found it...charming.

No, not charming. He'd pitied the girl once she realized her mistake.

To be fair, he had not realized her assumption until it was too late to set her straight. And when he *had* realized her mistake, he'd been...

Well, he wasn't sure what it was he'd felt. Amusement, perhaps. But it was something more than that. It had delighted him in a way few things had, the fact that she was speaking to him as though they were in on a secret.

As though he were a trusted friend or an intimate acquaintance.

"I will have a word with her," Mrs. Harper said, sounding as frazzled as she looked.

"No, no, I will do it," he said.

Both Mrs. Harper and Gregory wore similar expressions of wariness. He had to stifle an exasperated sigh. He was well aware that he had a reputation for being somewhat standoffish. Cold, even. But he'd never been *cruel*, particularly not with any members of his staff.

"You can both calm down," he said. "I have no intention of harming the girl or tossing her out on the streets. I merely wish to discover what it is that is troubling her."

And fix it.

He kept that last part to himself because he was certain it would surprise them as much as it did him. He wanted to solve whatever problem was going on in her life. But first he needed to get her out of his home and take her...where, exactly?

That was the most pressing question. He would deal with

whatever problems she was facing once he convinced her to trust him with her secrets—he'd slay her dragons, as it were—but in the meantime, what was to be done with the girl?

"I shall go fetch her," Mrs. Harper said, her tone still too nervous for his liking. He was perhaps a bit too gruff at times, but he wasn't an *ogre*, for goodness sake.

"I'll go to her," he said.

He wasn't sure why. Possibly because he knew he could find her in the crowded servants' quarters, surrounded by the safety of numbers. If she were to come here to him, he knew Gregory would give them privacy and Mrs. Harper would be the only thing standing between him and...

Between him and what, exactly?

His errant mind drew up an image of her lips as if on demand.

Yes, all right, perhaps he had experienced a pang of... temptation. He straightened his cravat impatiently as he strode toward the door. Stupid, ridiculous temptation. He'd had the thought that he should have liked to kiss her, and just like that, the notion had swept over him like a tidal wave. Something about her had gotten under his skin before he could steel himself against it.

Now it seemed that base desire still held him in its grip, which meant it was all the better that he was going to see her in the well-populated servants' quarters.

So now here he was, fleeing the comfort of his own study because he couldn't quite trust himself not to act on this ridiculous temptation.

He followed Mrs. Harper who scurried down the hallways toward the back staircase.

His reaction to her had clearly been an anomaly, and no doubt brought on by the strangeness of their first meeting. It wasn't as though he met many young ladies while they lie in his lap.

Yes, that was surely the cause of his problem. He'd been caught at a disadvantage by the strange intimacy of their first interaction. Now he would face her—upright and at a safe distance—and all would be right with the world.

After all, it wasn't as though the girl herself was so very tempting. She was no diamond of the first water. She'd been plain other than those lush lips and those sparkling blue eyes.

All right, fine, perhaps she was pretty.

But hardly irresistible.

It was these thoughts that had him marching confidently down the hallway, with Mrs. Harper at his side, toward the room he was told Addie shared with Betsy, one of the girls who helped Cook in the kitchen.

Mrs. Harper knocked, and when there was no answer, she cracked the door open. Then she pushed it all the way open, and Alec found himself gazing upon an empty room.

Not just empty.

Deserted.

It looked like it had been ransacked. Nothing adorned the nightstand, and some of the drawers were half open as though someone had left in a rush.

She ran.

He knew it just as surely as he knew that he would find her.

He hadn't been lying when he'd told Mrs. Harper that anyone in his employment was his responsibility. He might not have been an overly kind man, but he was nothing if not responsible. He saw to his obligations, and that included maids who fainted at his feet.

It had nothing to do with her pretty pink lips or those sparkling eyes when he raced back down the stairs and through the back entrance. He would have done the same for any staff member.

He caught up to her just as she was trying to slip out the

back gate, a sack slung over her shoulder like she was a thief in the night. "Where do you think you are going?"

He hadn't intended to scare the girl, but she jumped all the same, turning to face him with a decidedly guilty expression on her face. "I, uh, I..." Her shoulders slumped in defeat. "I was leaving."

Studying her here, now, in the afternoon light, with her standing upright rather than lying across his lap, he had a more objective view of her.

She was pretty, that was a fact. Her light brown hair shimmered with blonde and auburn highlights, and even from here, he could see the brilliant blue of her eyes. When he'd called her 'little one' earlier it had been because she'd seemed so young, so innocent. And now? Well she was still young and an air of sweet naiveté hung over her like a halo, but there was no denying the fact that she was a grown woman. Petite, yes, and too thin by far—but despite that, she had the form of a lady that not even that ugly brown shroud could hide.

Good heavens, did all of his employees dress like this? Like they were monks at a monastery required to wear burlap sacks as some sort of penance?

He made a note to talk to Mrs. Harper about the wages. Perhaps it was time for an increase.

Throughout all this scrutinizing, he was amused to realize that she was doing the same. She wasn't even trying to hide the fact that she was sizing him up from head to toe. He knew what she saw—tall, broad, dark hair and an expression that was more often than not described as brooding—a word which he despised. It made him sound like a romantic poet and not the respected member of society that he was.

He itched to go to her. To take her by the hand like the child she claimed not to be and drag her back into the house where he could protect her. At least until he sorted out whatever mess she'd gotten herself into.

It seemed she had other ideas.

"Please," she said softly. "Please, just let me leave. I won't cause you any more problems."

He frowned at that. "I'm afraid I cannot allow you to do that."

Her eyes, which had been wide with surprise and fear, narrowed suddenly in displeasure. "Cannot or will not?"

A smile tugged at his lips. Awfully feisty for such a small, frightened creature. It was the frightened part that concerned him. Whatever was wrong in her life, she clearly needed assistance, and he would hardly be a gentleman if he refused to aid a young lady in distress. He took a step forward but froze when she jerked back in alarm.

"I will not hurt you," he said, using the same voice he used to calm his horse during a thunderstorm. "I merely wish to offer my assistance."

She bit her lip, and he tried not to notice. He kept his eyes firmly locked on hers. He knew now from experience that one look at her lips could wreak havoc on his sanity. "Come," he said, nodding toward the back door to his home. "We will get you fed and then come up with a solution."

"A solution?" She sounded so wary he might as well have offered torture.

"Yes, a solution." He looked pointedly toward the back alley where she'd been headed. "The sun will be setting soon, and the streets are no place for a young lady alone."

She winced slightly, and he knew she recognized that he was right. Still, she hesitated. "I cannot stay here."

"No, you cannot," he said, perhaps a touch too firmly. "My home is no place for a young unwed lady such as yourself."

Interestingly, her cheeks started to turn a pale shade of pink—preferable to the extreme pale state he'd found her in earlier but alarming in its own right. Had her thoughts strayed to the same places his had gone? Unattached young lady and a notoriously eligible bachelor?

Was she worried that he'd attack her?

The very thought was disturbing. "I shan't hurt you, you know."

Even from where he stood several paces away, he could see her swallow. But he noticed she did not agree with him.

Who on earth had made this girl so wary of men? A hot, fiery rage swept through him as his mind went to all sort of dark places about what could have happened to her...worse, what still might if he did not make her see sense and accept his help.

"What is your real name, Miss Adelaide?" Curiosity had gotten the best of him, and he knew it was the wrong question as soon as it slipped out.

She pressed her lips together firmly and gave her head a little shake.

He sighed, running a hand through his hair and most likely mussing it thoroughly. "You might as well tell me, you know." He arched his brows. "I already know that you come from a good family. It would not be difficult to find out who is missing a daughter or..." He hesitated, for the first time realizing that perhaps he'd jumped to the wrong conclusion. "A wife?"

She frowned, and the look was adorably peevish. As though he were the exasperating one here, and not she.

He thought she might not answer, but finally she shifted her sack with a little huff. "I do not see why you should care, my lord. We have agreed that I am not welcome here."

"Not in my employ, no," he agreed. "I have no interest in harboring a runaway debutante who's had a rift with her family."

Her frown turned to a scowl. He'd hoped to irritate her with that comment, and it had worked. Now he had to fight another grin as she glared at him like a schoolmarm and he was a disobedient child.

He liked this side of her. Her anger was far preferable to her fear.

"I am not a debutante," she started.

"But you are also not a servant," he added. "Which means I do not know what you are, only that you do not belong here with me."

She flinched a bit, and he felt a pang of remorse. "If you tell me where your home is, I am certain—"

"I cannot go home." Her voice was hard. Firm. There was no room for argument. Still, she added. "I *will* not."

He hesitated only briefly before giving her a short nod. "Very well. I will not insist on taking you home."

She seemed to relax a bit, and he saw a world of weariness in her as her shoulders slumped beneath the weight of that sack. He supposed she was thinking the same thing as him. If she could not stay here and she could not go home...where was she to go?

He hated the despair that she could not quite hide, not even in her anger. It lingered in the back of her eyes and clung to her like a second skin.

"I will find a solution," he said. He'd sounded so confident that he even managed to convince himself. But, after all, he was a man of title, power, and wealth. Surely he could find some decent solution for a gently bred young lady with nowhere to go.

She was still eyeing him warily, and for a moment he wished he was more like his best friend, the Duke of Harlow. Royce was off on his honeymoon with his new bride, but right about now, Royce's easy charm would have been welcome. He'd know what to say to put this girl at ease—

And just like that, inspiration struck. The School of Charm. Owned by Lady Charmian and now being run by

Lady Harlow's closest friend—he should have thought of it at once.

Of course, they would accept her, and they would likely know what to do with the girl as well. Maybe they could even pry the truth out of her.

"Come along," he said, already turning to head back inside. "I know now what we shall do with you. Let us get you fed, and we'll be on our way."

CHAPTER 3

A ddie eyed the Earl over her bowl of broth.

She wished she could enjoy the bread and broth Cook had set before her at the kitchen table, but it was impossible when the Earl watched her like that with his arms crossed on the other side of the table.

She eyed him warily, half expecting him to rebuke her for not eating more quickly or something. He had an air of impatience about him. Likely because he couldn't wait to be rid of her. *I know what we shall do with you,* he'd said.

Like she was a package that had been misplaced or a stray cat that had been abandoned.

She sipped her broth. Neither was too far off the mark, she supposed, and yet her pride still stung a bit at being thought of as some nuisance that needed to be dealt with.

She was a nuisance. She knew she was. But it still smarted.

Mrs. Harper's arrival in the kitchen finally had him looking away from her, and Addie could at last take a large bite of the bread without feeling like the helpless, starving waif he seemed to see her as.

She sniffed. *Runaway debutante, indeed.*

"Have you sent word?" he asked Mrs. Harper.

"Yes, my lord. I had the footman wait for a response." She handed the Earl a note that he unfolded and read, not seeming to notice or care that his secretiveness was driving her mad.

I know what we shall do with you.

Ever since he'd made that declaration he'd been moving about with determination, not deigning to tell Addie of his plans for her. And why should he? She supposed she ought to be grateful that he was even taking an interest.

And yet, whatever plan he had in mind...it would not work.

He was not aware of the entirety of her situation, and he didn't know the most important part. Reggie. No matter where he took her, she'd only have to leave.

She held back a sigh and focused on her food, wondering how much bread she might be able to tuck into her pockets for Reggie without the Earl noticing.

She eyed him across the table as he read the missive.

The man was too attentive by far. She had a feeling nothing would get past him, not even a stray crumb going into her pocket.

"Excellent," he said as he placed the note down on the table. He wasn't talking to her, merely to himself, or maybe to Mrs. Harper. She seemed to be an afterthought in whatever plan he was concocting.

She thought to ask him if perhaps she ought to have a say in wherever she was shipped off to, but held her tongue. She should be grateful for his interest. It was hardly *his* fault she was in this situation, and he was under no obligation to help her. He could have put her out on her ear if he'd seen fit.

Maybe he *should* have.

She wasn't his problem, and Reggie certainly didn't fall under his care. As far as she knew, her father never even knew the Earl of Tolston, so he certainly owed nothing to her family.

None of it was his responsibility.

The fault for her sad state fell entirely on the shoulders of Duncan, her cousin, her guardian, and the reason she could never go home again. Duncan who'd swept into their lives the moment her father had passed and taken over full control of the estate.

It was his right; she understood that. The will had given him full control—though the majority of the money had been put into a trust, to be given to Reggie when he was older. Or, in the tragic event of Reggie's death, to the next heir of Wrencliff—Duncan.

It wasn't his eagerness to take guardianship that had frightened her. It was his ill-disguised desire to be the heir to her father's title and all that went with it.

She'd been so grief-stricken when Duncan had first arrived that she'd been quiet. Silent, even. Duncan seemed to assume she was deaf as well as dumb because he talked—loudly and enthusiastically—to his friends and his solicitor, all of whom took up residence in her home. He talked about how he ought to be the heir. About how her mother had no business having another child so late in life. How he'd lived his life assuming that he'd be entailed the property, the title... the fortune.

It hadn't taken much digging to discover exactly what he'd meant by that.

He was up to his ears in debt.

Worse, it was soon apparent that his mental health was questionable, to say the least. His moods were fickle and extreme, and there were times he'd looked at her with wild eyes that had made her feel frozen to the bone. He'd looked possessed by an evil spirit.

And then in the third week after his arrival, it had begun.

He'd shoved her when he was drunk, he'd raised a fist to one of the footmen, but worst of all—he'd gripped her brother so hard he'd had bruises on his arms for days.

That was when she started to truly fear him. But it wasn't until she'd overheard him speaking to one of his friends one night when she ought to have been in bed that her fear had turned to panic.

"You can still have it all," his friend had said. She'd never seen the man, but his voice was that of the devil himself. Cold and merciless. *"You are next in line after the boy, no?"*

He'd been met with silence, which she'd stupidly taken to be a horror akin to what she was feeling. The stranger couldn't honestly have been suggesting what she thought he'd been suggesting.

"Think about it," the stranger had said, his voice cajoling, his tone so cruel she'd shivered where she'd stood. "Accidents happen all the time to little children."

More silence. She'd waited for Duncan to protest. To laugh, even, because surely this was a joke.

"You're right. It would be easy enough to be rid of the boy." Duncan didn't laugh. He didn't sound like he was joking. He sounded...serious. Thoughtful. Like he was actually thinking it over. From that moment on, she'd watched her cousin closely and saw just how deranged he truly was.

Reggie's nursemaid was sent away for no reason two days later, and when she'd asked him why, he'd responded with a blow. Casually, not even in anger, he'd backhanded her and sent her flying. His fits of violent rage grew worse over the next few weeks, and while she tried her best to protect Reggie from their cousin, she'd not been able to spare him all of Duncan's cruelty.

It was when she caught Duncan alone in her sleeping brother's room that she knew without a doubt that she had to leave and take Reggie with her.

The problem was, she'd had nowhere to go.

While she'd seen the truth about Duncan, the rest of the world was blind. Duncan had a reputation for being the life of every party. He was all laughter and kind words when they had visitors, and everyone walked away from him with a smile on their faces, cheered just by being near him.

She'd written letters to several distant relatives and family friends, but the few responses she received chalked her fears up to her grief. They thought she was having a hard time adjusting to a new guardian. That perhaps he was stricter with her than her own father had been.

Perhaps she should have been clearer—maybe she should have spelled out his actions. But after being met with silence or platitudes, she hadn't the heart. Not to mention, time was running out. Everything in her knew it. It screamed for her to leave with Reggie while they still could.

While Reggie still lived.

She might have been paranoid to believe he'd resort to murder, but it was a chance she was not willing to take.

One distant cousin seemed to believe her, but she was a spinster with no power to help. Still, Emmaline Haversham did what she could by hiding her here at the Earl's home. Telling her about the position and sending a reference.

And now...

She eyed the Earl again as he folded the note carefully. He was back to watching her like a hawk. She pushed the bowl away. Hungry as she was, she couldn't bring herself to take another bit under that fierce stare. He made her too uncomfortable. Humiliation still burned in her at the way she'd begged him not to tell the Earl.

What a fool.

He must have been laughing at her.

And now he thought to save her.

"Are you finished?" he asked, eyeing the food that was still in front of her.

She nodded. The sooner she got this over with, the sooner she could get to Reggie.

What then?

That she did not know. Perhaps Emmaline would help find her a new position, if she could find a way to get word to her. Or maybe Emmaline could convince her father to let them stay until they figure out where to go next. Maybe Emmaline's father would believe her word against Duncan's...

Unlikely since Emmaline had told her that Duncan was a favorite of her father's. And Emmaline's father was a distant relative of hers; he barely knew her—certainly not well enough to believe her word over Duncan's.

"Shall we?"

She looked up in surprise to see the Earl standing beside her, a hand out to help her from her seat. She took it his hand but kept her head tucked down, slipping her fingers out from his the moment she was standing.

"Mrs. Harper, tell Gregory to dine without me. I might be a while." He strode toward the door, clearly expecting her to follow.

They might be a while? How far was this place he planned to take her?

It wasn't until they were in his carriage that she summoned the courage to ask. "Where exactly are you taking me?"

The sun was starting to set, and the shadows in the carriage made him look dangerous as he flashed in and out of the light. Even so, she felt safer here with this veritable stranger than with her cousin.

"Have you heard of the Earl of Charmian?"

She nodded. The Earl of Charm was his nickname. She'd never met the man herself, but she knew the name.

"His wife opened a School of Charm," he continued.

Her brows hitched up at that. "A School of *Charm?*"

His lips twitched slightly in a way she was starting to recognize. It meant he was amused, and likely trying not to laugh at her. "Yes, a finishing school for young ladies."

Her brows drew down in confusion. "I cannot pay for finishing school." She shifted in her seat. She did not *need* finishing school—after all, what good would it be to improve her embroidery or practice her French when she'd left society behind along with her dowry and her home?

He was watching her with that serious expression of his. *Grim.* Yes, she could see why people called him that now, though she suspected it was just the way he looked. Like the Grim Reaper. She might have had a childish air about her, but he looked as though he'd struck a deal with the devil. Though she had a sense that there was so much more to him.

In fact, she'd seen it for herself. Despite the lazy way he slouched back in this carriage seat and the heavy-lidded stare that saw everything, she still recalled the warmth in his eyes when he'd taken care of her earlier that day. She recalled in vivid detail the kindness in his eyes.

"I appreciate the thought," she said stiffly. "But I do not have the money for tuition or—"

"There is no need to pay," he said now.

She bit her lip. "So, I could work there?"

Hope flickered. Perhaps she could continue the same arrangement—working as a servant and paying old Mrs. Grishna to watch Reggie while she saved her coins to afford a home of their own.

She could do this. All was not lost. A smile started to form until he continued. "I will pay your tuition."

She blinked. "Pardon me?"

He leaned forward suddenly, and she remembered tales she'd heard of large cats in the jungle that would lie in wait and then pounce. He moved like that—all cynical laziness and apathy until he struck with a sudden intensity. Now he was so close she could smell his scent—something male and divine that made her feel warm and safe even as her heart thudded wildly at his proximity.

"You will be in their charge," he said. "For the time being."

She leaned back, trying to get enough distance that she might wrap her head around this turn of events. "For the time being?"

His gaze was even. "Yes. Until we find your family and sort out whatever mess you've gotten yourself into."

She blinked in shock before looking away out the window of the carriage. She wasn't certain why she was hurt. If her own friends and family had not taken her pleas for help seriously, there was no reason to expect a stranger to trust that she'd had good reason to flee her home.

"Perhaps Miss Grayson will be able to get through to you," he said.

"Miss Grayson?" she repeated quietly, still looking away, still hurt beyond reason. How was it that right now she felt more alone than she had this morning? It did not make sense.

"A friend of mine," he answered. "Lord Charmian opened the school along with his wife, but they've recently had a child and Miss Grayson was put in charge of the day to day running of the establishment."

Addie nodded mutely, uncertain what she was supposed to say to that. She was slightly curious what he thought Miss Grayson might be able to accomplish, or why he thought she would spill her troubles to a strange lady. But in the end, she kept quiet, because in the end...it did not matter.

She would not stay.

She couldn't.

They might accept her as a charge, but what of Reggie?

And if she could not earn a wage, she could not pay for him to be taken care of.

"You look troubled." Somehow he made this sound like an accusation.

She turned back to him, hoping he could not read her emotions. "Thank you for your assistance, my lord. You have gone above and beyond your duty."

She'd meant to be kind, to say the right thing, and yet now he was frowning at her like she'd offended him.

"I did no such thing. I am merely doing right by one who is under my charge."

She pressed her lips together in annoyance. He made it sound like she was his child, just like he'd spoken to her like she was one earlier that day.

"As I said, I appreciate your assistance." She tried to mean it. It wasn't his fault that his meddling in her affairs would only make matters worse for her. She'd been doing just fine working at his home, paying Mrs. Grishna with food she could sneak out and a little coin, and now she would be forced to start anew.

But again, it was not his fault. It was her own stupid fault for fainting like a ninny at his house, and for telling him the truth about her station. She had no one else to blame.

"You know..." He leaned back once more and his tone turned lazy and slow. "If you were to tell me what happened to you at your home, I might be able to be of more assistance."

"I thank you, my lord," she said stiffly as she stared pointedly out the window. "But I assure you, there is no need."

"Did someone hurt you?" His abrupt question and the anger behind it had her inhaling too quickly and too loudly. She cursed herself for stiffening and forced herself to relax. The last thing she needed was an Earl to get involved. For all she knew, he was a friend of Duncan's. Everyone she'd met seemed to be. With that thought she forced a small smile of regret. "It is as you guessed, my lord. I have merely run away after a tiff with my parents. I am sure we shall set things right eventually."

His eyes glimmered with something dangerous—a heady mix of amusement and curiosity. It was impossible to look away.

"How odd," he said. "One would think that you'd be a better liar than this."

She frowned. She'd done a fine job of lying...hadn't she? Also, how dare he call her a liar?

"But then again, you couldn't even recall your fabricated surname," he continued in that low drawl that made her insides flutter.

She bit her lip at the reminder. She ought to let it go. The less said the better. And yet... "You caught me at a low moment, my lord."

His quick lopsided grin, there and gone in a heartbeat, made her entire body go into a state of shock. "Indeed. I ought not to have taken advantage of your obvious distress by asking you for your *name*...Miss Adelaide."

His voice dripped with sarcasm, but it did not seem unkind. She felt a smile tugging her own lips until she squashed the urge. She should not encourage his teasing. Instead, she turned to face the window again as the carriage began to slow.

"So," he continued. "You did not run away over some trivial family rift. I thought not, but I had to be sure."

She whipped her head around to gape at him. "You are trying to provoke me."

His smirk held no regret. "If you won't tell me what's going on, I'll do whatever I must to get to the bottom of this."

"Why?" she shot back. "Why do you care?"

She regretted the words instantly. Of course, he didn't care. That wasn't what she'd meant. She'd merely meant...why would he not let her be?

He regarded her for a long moment as the carriage stilled beside a large building of gray stone. "I'm not entirely sure."

He said it so quietly she nearly didn't hear him. It was more to himself than to her, and before she could respond, he was opening the carriage door and helping her down. He stayed by her side as a butler greeted them at the door, and sat beside her on a settee as they awaited Miss Grayson in a drawing room that was comfortable and lovely.

Homey, even.

Addie took in the space with a mix of longing and regret. If it was only her on the run, she'd be all too happy to stay in a place such as this. Not nearly so fine and grand as the Earl's townhouse. It was stately and fine, but it had a woman's touch and it felt welcoming. Even now, a fire burned to fight the chill in the air this spring evening, and she longed to curl up beside it and sleep away her troubles.

She stiffened at the thought. Now was hardly the time to be tempted by luxuries. The Earl glanced over at her, as he'd been prone to do since they arrived. She ignored the curious looks that he hid so well behind that lazy façade.

It *was* a façade, she was beginning to realize. He looked so at ease, but he was always watching, always thinking. She had the nervous sensation that he was also always *plotting*.

Plotting what? She had no idea. But this particular evening, his scheming seemed to be entirely fixed on her.

When a maid announced that the Miss Grayson was on her way, Addie sighed with relief. At least now she could get on with it. She could nod her agreement, pretend to be docile until the Earl finally left and washed his hands of her.

Her eyes darted to the door when it opened again, and her eyes widened with surprise. She was not certain what she had expected of Miss Grayson—perhaps someone befitting the word 'gray' in her name. But this lady was neither elderly nor dull. She was...well, she was spectacularly beautiful, there was no other way to describe her.

Tall, with silvery blonde hair, she looked like she ought to be a queen, or perhaps a duchess, or maybe even a princess from a fairy tale. Her slim build was sheathed in a plain green gown, but even so she shone like a jewel.

She would have been intimidating if her gaze when she turned to Adelaide had not been filled with such kindness. "Welcome," she'd said gently, taking Addie's hands in her own and squeezing. "I am so glad you have come."

Addie's lips tugged up in a smile. The lady had said it so sincerely, for a moment there she'd nearly believed her.

When Miss Grayson turned to the Earl, she caught the smile they shared. Something small and secretive. Addie felt a stab of...something.

Loneliness, she supposed. When they walked a few feet away and shared a few murmured words, it was clear that they had a friendship, of sorts.

She tried not to stare at them, looking down at her own faded, shoddy frock instead. Whatever this sensation was when she watched Tolston talking like a normal human being and not like some stodgy Earl...she didn't like it.

The sooner he left, the better.

And yet, when he came over to wish her a stilted and cold goodbye, she was not relieved. Not at all. She could not quite bring herself to meet his eyes as he looked down at her. She wasn't sure whether she wished to see that warmth she'd seen earlier or if she was terrified to see it—she knew from experience what havoc it wreaked on her. And so, she kept her gaze on his chin.

A lovely chin it was, too. He had a small cleft, and the shadow of facial hair at this late hour gave him a rather dashing, dangerous air. For a moment she could tell herself he was a pirate or a highwayman—not the great, noble, upstanding Earl of Tolston with his grand house and his plentiful staff and his long-awaited pursuit of a wife.

Now, why had she gone and thought about that?

He went to turn away after wishing her the best, but seemed to hesitate. "You can trust Miss Grayson."

Surprise had her gaze darting up to meet his.

Mistake. It was a huge mistake. One look, and she felt like he could read all of her secrets. Worse, she saw that blasted warmth again—the sweet, tender affection that seemed to lurk beneath the surface.

It was that warmth that had made her cry like a fool earlier, and she hated the fact that she longed to give in to that urge again now. What a relief it would be to throw herself into his arms and weep. What a temptation it was to let this man with his strong shoulders and his grim expression deal with all the problems in her life.

She'd never much gone for tales of knights or dashing princes who saved the damsel in distress, but looking into the Earl's eyes right now?

She was beginning to understand the appeal.

"Thank you for your assistance, my lord," she said with as much humility as she could muster. She dropped into a low curtsy, which was not only polite, but spared her the pain of having to meet his gaze any longer.

"Miss Grayson will take good care of you." He sounded like he was reassuring himself as much as her.

When he left, the air felt cooler but she was once more able to breathe freely. Miss Grayson was all that was kind and hospitable as she showed her to her room and had a tray of food sent for.

"The rest of the girls are so excited to meet you," she said as she fussed about the small but pretty room, making it even more comfortable. "I told them they'd have to wait until the morning after you've had a chance to rest."

Addie forced as smile in return. The rest of the girls? She wondered how many, and what had brought them here to this house. But she would not ask. For then, Miss Grayson might take that to mean that she too could ask questions.

Addie appreciated the fact that she did not pry, although before she left her room, Miss Grayson turned back with that warm smile. "Perhaps in the morning after you are fed and rested, you'll feel comfortable enough to talk, hmm?"

Addie's expression remained the same. An answering smile that said nothing at all. That seemed to suffice for Miss Grayson, and she took her leave.

She moved to make herself comfortable—she had hours yet before she could escape unnoticed, but before she'd settled in, there was a soft knock on the door, followed by a pretty redhead poking her head into the room. "Hello."

Addie blinked in surprise.

The girl didn't wait for a response or a welcome before sneaking in, peering down the hallway quickly before darting into the room and partially closing the door behind her. "I'm Louisa," she said, her smile bright and welcoming. With a small curtsy, she added, "Miss Louisa Purchase. Who are you?"

"I—that is—" She let out a huff of exasperation. Tolston had been right. She truly was a terrible liar. "Miss Adelaide Tillman," she said.

"You must call me Louisa," the redhead said. "Miss Grayson said we ought to give you space until morning, but I just wanted to say hello and make sure you knew how welcome you are." She grinned, and Addie found herself smiling back at the other young woman. It seemed almost impossible not to. "We were all so pleased to hear we'll have some more company." She leaned forward and lowered her voice. "And a new lady who's mired in mystery," she said in a hushed voice that didn't disguise her glee. "All the better."

Addie was torn between laughter and tears. Louisa made it sound as though her hardships were something lovely and romantic. They weren't. Not at all.

And yet, the girl's optimism and enthusiasm were sweet, and her expressive eyes were filled with heart.

"Thank you," she said softly. "I'm pleased to meet you."

At least there she didn't have to lie. This girl seemed lovely. It was too bad she couldn't get to know her better.

Louisa backed away toward the door. "I'll let you get your rest. But if you need anything—anything at all—please do let me know."

"I will, thank you," she said, her own voice just as quiet.

When Louisa walked out and shut the door behind her, Addie had to brace herself against a wave of longing. How lovely it would be to stay here indefinitely. To have a motherly figure in Miss Grayson, and maybe even a friend in Louisa...

But that was just a daydream. Not her reality. She took a deep breath and locked the door behind Louisa. Best not to let her mind wonder about things that could not be.

She looked out the window and watched the sun setting over the buildings across the way. No, it was no use longing for things she could never have, and a home here was one of them. An image of the Earl of Tolston flashed through her mind so fast and fierce it left her breathless. Those eyes, that smirk, the way he'd held her in his arms...

She blinked the image away. Just another glimpse of all that she could not have. She had only one person to think about right now, and he'd be waiting for her to arrive.

She turned away from the window and went back to the bed to get some rest while she could. She had a long night ahead of her and very little idea of where she would turn next.

To Emmaline, she supposed. Her relative would help keep them fed and sheltered until they could come up with another solution. She just had to hope Emmaline's parents didn't find out and send her back.

Addie stared up at the ceiling and tried not to think. She tried not to cry. She tried not to think about *what ifs* and *if onlys*. None of those did her any good, because her future wasn't here, and it certainly wasn't one that involved the Earl of Tolston. Her future was hazy and terrifying, but she did know one thing...

Once the house was asleep, she'd be gone.

CHAPTER 4

Fresh air, that was what he needed.

Alec walked quickly down the streets of his neighborhood, which were remarkably quiet at this time of night. He wasn't one to take a stroll, not even on a pleasant spring evening like this one, but he'd been driven out of his own house by this overwhelming sense of unease.

He was unsettled, which was also not like him.

It hadn't helped that Mrs. Harper had fussed all evening about 'the poor girl.' But even without Mrs. Harper's nagging and Gregory's relentless questions, he had a feeling he'd still be thinking about her.

He found himself replaying every word she'd spoken, every touch, every look, every smile. All in some vain attempt to figure out her secrets. He'd asked Gregory if he'd heard about any missing daughters from high society homes in London, but he'd been just as clueless.

How could a young lady like her go missing without everyone knowing about it?

And why could he not shake the feeling that she was not

well when he'd left her. She'd smiled, she'd said all the right things. She'd been civil, subservient, and docile.

Perhaps *too* docile.

He gave his head a shake and buried his hands in his pockets as he tried to figure out what it was about her that was nagging at him...

Aside from her lips.

And her eyes.

And her hair.

He groaned and tilted his head back to look up at the cloudless sky. This was why he'd needed to clear his head. Fresh air was exactly what he needed.

The sound of a hackney approaching had him turning to stare. It was late, and few people were out on the streets. It was traveling in the same direction that he was.

It stopped a few houses down, and when a young lady emerged, he stopped.

Now he was certain. Miss Addie Adelaide had bewitched him. That was the only reason he'd be seeing her now, in the dead of night, more than ten blocks away from his own home and far from Miss Grayson's School of Charm, where he'd left her.

And yet...

He stared in fascination at the young woman wrapped an ugly black shawl over an even uglier brown shroud that was too familiar. Even from yards away and in the dark of night, he could see a glimmer in her hair from the moonlight. Her head was tilted down, but he recognized the pointed chin, the pert nose, the eyes that seemed too big for her face.

And then there was that sack, hanging over her shoulder.

He let out his breath on a shaky exhale.

It was her.

Adelaide.

And she'd run.

But what on earth was she doing *here*? He opened his mouth to call out to her but stopped short. If he shouted, she would run. How did he know this? He wasn't sure, but there was no doubt in his mind. This was the second time she'd run, and whatever had brought her here—on her own and in the middle of the night?

Well, something told him this was at the heart of her secrets.

And whether he liked it or not, Alec desperately wanted to know her secrets.

He watched in silent fascination as Miss Addie Adelaide —what a ridiculous name—made her way hastily up the steps and knocked on a door. Clearly shivering, she glanced from side to side before knocking again. Banging loudly this time as she huddled in on herself.

It wasn't a cold night, but there was a chill in the air that her thin shawl would do nothing to stop. He started toward her. This was ridiculous. He could not just stand here watching her shiver.

Whatever it was that had drawn her from the comfortable and safe confines of Miss Grayson's school, it could hardly be worth freezing to death. He'd gone three paces when the door opened. An elderly woman poked her head out, and while he could not hear what was said, he'd have bet his entire fortune that the stranger was chastising Adelaide, who'd hunched in on herself as she nodded meekly, her hands clasped together in a plea.

What on earth?

Alec straightened his shoulders and strode toward her with more confidence. Whatever was going on here, it was time he intervened. He was an Earl, for heaven's sake. If Miss Adelaide needed assistance, surely he was the one to—

His mind went blank as a young child was unceremoniously thrust across the doorway. The elderly woman pushed

47

the youngster into Adelaide's arms, and she held the thing close.

What the—

And then it all clicked into place. It all became clear.

The girl had gotten pregnant. She'd run away from home and had a babe out of wedlock.

His heart twisted painfully in his chest at the thought of this girl on her own. The door slammed shut in her face, and she turned to leave, the child clutched tight.

Alec's chest tightened again at the sight of Adelaide with a child in her arms. Where was she going? What did she plan to do?

She paused there on the sidewalk, and he had the feeling she was wondering the same thing. Her indecision did away with his own, and he strode toward her, noting her jolt of surprise and fear when she heard him approach.

He didn't miss the moment when she registered who was walking in her directions. Her feelings about seeing him were clear. Very clear.

She was horrified.

Shocked, yes, but there was a distinct flare of horror in her eyes, as though she feared him.

Him. The one who'd tried to save her. Her horror had him clenching his jaw in irritation, and he needed no mirror to know that his heavy brow was drawn down in a fierce scowl.

He hadn't the energy to care.

"What are you doing here?" Addie asked, her voice breathless with shock as she clutched her child tighter.

"What am *I* doing here?" It came out through clenched teeth. But really, of all the foolish, naïve actions... "Do you have any idea how dangerous the streets are to young ladies alone at this time of night?"

Her head jerked back in shock at the anger in his voice that he didn't try to hide. She drew herself up to her full height. "I hardly believe Mayfair is the most dangerous neighborhood in London, my lord."

He stalked closer and watched with a flicker of admiration as she tilted her chin up and held his stare. Most grown men would have gone running by now. But not this young lady... His eyes fell to the babe in her arms, a fat little thing with chubby cheeks and eyes that drooped as though he were seconds away from sleep.

Maybe because she was a mother she had more nerve than most. Or maybe it came from how she was raised. He eyed her from head to toe, not bothering to hide his interest.

She intrigued him, was that so wrong?

Yes! A voice of reason told him just how wrong that was. He was in town for the season to find a wife, start a family—not rescue fallen women and their bastard children.

"Where do you think you're going?" he asked.

She licked her lips, and he could not look away. His body grew warm with wanting even as his heart did that painful twist that was really starting to become quite irksome. He hated seeing her look so nervous. So desperate. It did things to him. It made him feel things that he had no place feeling.

In no world should he feel so possessive of a young lady who meant nothing to him—who *could* mean nothing to him.

He wasn't some romantic fool—his best friend Royce had always played that role. He was the pragmatic one. The *cynical* one. The one who never lost his head, let alone his heart. He thought through his actions and moved through life making careful, calculated decisions while his friends lived for depravity and diversions.

"I have a place to go," she said.

"Do you?"

She blinked and pressed her lips together. She wasn't certain. She had an idea, that much was clear, but she did not know for certain. He could only imagine the worries she was facing. Would she be welcome? Would there be a room? Would she have enough money for food?

Every thought made his ribcage feel too small. Anger coursed through him, and he accepted it happily. Anger was so much easier to deal with than this absurd worry for a near-stranger's welfare.

"You're coming with me," he snapped, turning before she could argue. "Again."

He didn't hear her move, and after he'd gone a few steps he stopped. "You can either go with me now, or I will track you down in the morning."

Her quick intake of air was hard to decipher. Had he shocked her with the threat? Or was it anger that he'd spoken to her so. He didn't care either way. "I have a feeling Miss... what was her name? Miss Haversham? I feel confident she'd be able to help me locate you should you run away for a third time."

This time when he strode away, he heard her scurry after him. A true gentleman would have shortened his strides, but Alec was too angry. "What were you thinking?" he spat out a little while later as they turned onto his street.

"I can explain—"

"You could have been killed. You could have been hurt or—"

"But I wasn't."

It was the worst thing she could say. He spun to face her, and he had to force back a growl of rage in the face of her open face, her sweet naiveté, at the sheer injustice of a world that had left her standing here with *him*, with no better options.

"Who did this to you?" He gestured a hand toward the baby.

She blinked at him as if in incomprehension. "My lord, I—"

"Who left you this position?" he said. He was definitely growling now, and he watched her eyes widen in alarm. "I will not hurt you." He said it as calmly as he could. "But I will kill him."

This was likely not the best way to reassure her, but he'd long since lost his battle with reason. He blamed it on the late hour or the drink he'd had before he'd left the house. Whatever it was, he was clearly not in his right mind as he leaned down so his face was close to hers. "Tell me who fathered this child, and I shall have him drawn and quartered."

She blinked so rapidly he thought she might start to cry. But instead, he caught the hint of a smile. A huff of air, almost like a hysterical little laugh. "I can't...that is, I don't—"

"Do not try to protect the swine," he snapped. "Whoever takes advantage of a young innocent girl like yourself and then leaves her to fend for herself..." He shook his head, trying to regain sanity and failing miserably. "And your parents. What do they have to say for themselves?"

He saw her grow pale in the moonlight. "My parents are dead, my lord."

He cursed under his breath. And then he cursed again, louder this time. Then he turned to her once more. "I am sorry for your loss."

"Thank you," she said. Then she added with a soft sigh, "Me too."

Her answer was so simple, so sincere—it finally broke through his anger, and he felt it seep away as he tore off his overcoat in jerky movements and draped it over her and the child. "Come inside."

"I shouldn't," she said. "I appreciate that you wish to help me, but my situation it is...it is *complicated*."

He let out a huff of rueful amusement. "Complicated, eh? Maybe for a sheltered girl from a good home, but I assure you, you are hardly the first young lady to have, er..." He nodded toward the child. "To find oneself in a predicament."

She stared at him for a second before bursting out in a laugh. She clapped her hand over her mouth, and her eyes widened as she shook her head as though she too could not believe she was laughing.

For a moment he found his own lips twitching with amusement as he watched her battle a million emotions, all of which seemed to be coming out in the form of laughter, even as tears brimmed her eyes.

"I'm sorry," she said on a gasp.

He narrowed his gaze, his lips still quirked up in a grin. "Are you laughing or crying?"

"Both?" She shrugged, nudging the baby in the process so he lifted his little blond head and peered at his mother in curiosity. The child's mouth spread wide in a toothless grin as he laughed, which seemed to make his mother laugh even harder, which then made him laugh.

"This is not a humorous situation," she said at last, swiping at her eyes.

"No," he said sobering instantly. "Indeed, it is not."

"Lord Tolston, I understand that you mean well," she started.

"You will stay here."

She blinked at him, but he was certain her surprise could not have been any greater than his. "You said yourself, I cannot—"

He held up a hand. "Just for tonight."

The fear in her eyes was very nearly his undoing. "I cannot leave Reggie."

He sighed as he eyed the child. "Reggie, eh? Pleasure to meet you, Reggie. Welcome to my home."

The child cooed as Adelaide shifted him to her other hip. "But—but I could not ask—"

"You are not asking, and I am not offering," he said in his best Earl voice. The one that made grown men quake.

She arched her brows in surprise, and he could have sworn her lips twitched with suppressed amusement. "Then you are...*ordering* me to stay here. With you. With my child?"

He pressed his lips together in annoyance at the way she said it. Her amusement was equally irritating and admirable. Once again he was struck by the enigma before him—a lady so sweet and naïve, yet one who'd also born a child. A lady so frightened and wary, and yet unafraid to look him in the eyes and...and *tease* him.

A lady who'd been so weak she'd fainted at his feet, and yet she braved the streets and a life of hardship to care for this child. He made a note to ask her who that woman had been—or better still, he'd have Gregory look into it.

Yes, he'd have Gregory use his charm to dig for information. And when he was done interrogating the old lady—kindly, of course. Gregory could kill with his kindness. Then he'd set him on Miss Emmaline Haversham.

It was clear that young lady knew something. Perhaps if he gathered some more pieces to this puzzle, it would all become clear.

Alec met her curious stare as she eyed him with a bravery that belied her wariness.

Maybe if he figured out the puzzle, he'd stop being so fascinated with Miss Adelaide.

"We are clear then," he said. "You and Reggie will stay here tonight. Tomorrow you will return to Miss Grayson's school—"

"But Reggie—"

"We will find a place for Reggie." He glowered down at her. "Neither myself nor Miss Grayson is as cruel as you seem to think."

"I do not think—"

"You will stay." His voice was sharper than intended because all his earlier fears were back—all that might have happened to her. What he might have lost...

Stupidity, all of it.

Still, he leaned down until his nose nearly brushed hers. "Know this, Miss Addie Adelaide. If you run, I shall find you."

CHAPTER 5

Addie fretted with the edge of her bedsheet, listening to the soft, even sound of Reggie's breathing softly beside her.

One thing was clear. She would have to run.

She turned her head to face the sleeping child. Not tonight, obviously. They both needed to rest. Her heart ached at the sight of his sweet little face. What she was going to do with him now, she had no idea, but, despite that—she'd felt relief when Mrs. Grishna had handed him over to her tonight.

Mrs. Grishna had been angry because she'd been so late to arrive with her money and the extra food, but Addie hadn't heard a word of the rant once Reggie was in her arms. His warm solid weight on her should have felt like an anchor—without him in her life she might have been able to stay at that lovely school. Maybe even gotten her second chance in society somehow. Miss Grayson's had been tempting, and a little part of her would love nothing more than to believe she could go back to that life. But after all she'd been through, going to balls and marrying for love...it seemed like a silly childish dream.

Besides, without Reggie, she had no one.

She'd take life as a scullery maid with her little family over a lifetime of parties alone any day.

But how? Her stomach did that thing it now loved to do, churning like the sea as every doubt and fear swept through her.

How would she manage now?

How would she provide for Reggie?

She took a deep breath and held it. It was not fair, she decided. She was exhausted and wished for nothing more than the sweet relief of sleep...and yet now was the time when her mind chose to ask every question she could not answer.

On top of that, her stomach growled. Lord Tolston had tried to force some food into her and Reggie when they'd first arrived—he'd woken Mrs. Harper who'd fussed over her and Reggie like a mother hen.

It had been sweet, really. She'd always respected Mrs. Harper, but she'd never seen her like that before—all motherly concern and doting sing-song tones for Reggie. But Reggie had been falling asleep in her arms, far too exhausted for food, and she'd insisted on going with him.

She'd offered to go to her old room, but both Tolston and Mrs. Harper had insisted on her using one of the lavish guest rooms so there'd be more room for the two of them.

She looked over at Reggie who was sprawled haphazardly in his sleep. They'd had a point, she supposed. But being in this luxurious room...it only added to her unease.

She didn't belong here. It felt far too much like her old life, the one she'd walked away from. Maybe that was why she could not sleep. Being here in this room was only adding to her confusion about who she was and the life she was meant to have.

She'd given up all those old dreams when she'd left, and then...

Her mind flashed on an image of Lord Tolston, glaring down at her. The intensity in his eyes, that spark of fear that she'd caught there. Almost like he'd cared about her safety.

About *her*.

Utter hogwash. She threw the covers aside with a quick jerk, slipping out of bed with a new sense of urgency. She needed to move. To act. If she were to lay there one more second, she'd drive herself crazy with all these errant thoughts.

The nice thing about having worked in the home where one currently was a guest was that she knew her way around. In bare feet, she padded silently through the hallways and down the grand staircase.

The vaulted ceilings seemed to echo with the sound of her footsteps as she stole down the hallway toward the kitchen. Once there she took a deep breath of relief. Oddly enough, she felt more comfortable here with the still smoldering fire and the smells of the day's cooking than she had in the elegant guest room.

She saw some bread sitting out and went over to it.

She hadn't felt at ease in this kitchen as a servant, and she didn't feel at ease as a visitor...perhaps she'd never find a place where she truly felt she belonged, but she could at least ease her hunger.

That was a start.

She reached for a knife and began to cut off a hunk.

"If you are running again, you are doing a poor job of it." Tolston's low voice made her squeak in alarm as she whipped around, the knife in front of her.

He eyed it with a smirk that made her knees grow weak. "Are you threatening me in my own home?" His brows arched. "And with a *bread* knife?"

She looked down at the blade and then dropped it to her side quickly. "You startled me."

"I might say the same." He crossed his arms as he fixed her with a glower. "Were you running away?"

She looked down pointedly at her night rail and arched her brows just as he had.

"Very well." He gave a huff of amusement. "Couldn't sleep, then?"

She shook her head.

"Too hungry?" By the amusement that tinged his voice, she suspected he knew very well that hunger wasn't all of it.

"That and I fear my mind has a way of racing away without me at night," she admitted.

His lips quirked up on one side in a look that was positively dangerous. She found herself holding her breath for no good reason.

"Welcome to the club," he said, lifting his right hand which held a glass filled with an amber liquid. "Come," he said, nodding toward the hallway where he'd just arrived. "Grab your little meal and join me."

"Oh, I could not—"

"I insist." His tone brooked no argument and he turned and walked away before she could try.

With a weary sigh, she finished cutting the bread, found herself a plate and poured a large glass of milk. When she could dawdle no longer, she followed in his path with the plate and glass in hand.

He was easy to find—the only door open with a glow coming from within. Still, she paused in the doorway.

"Come in," he ordered.

She wasn't sure whether to be amused or annoyed that he only spoke to her in commands.

"So," he said when she'd settled in on the large leather

seat across from him, tucking her legs beneath her as she dug in to her food. "What is it that has you up all night?"

She sighed as she chewed. Was it not obvious?

He didn't wait for her answer. "I told you I would make sure you and your child are safe."

She swallowed thickly and the bread seemed to lodge in her throat. She coughed around it as her eyes watered. She supposed she still hadn't quite gotten used to hearing Reggie referred to as her child.

She still couldn't believe her initial reaction was to *laugh*. Even when it hinged on the hysterical, laughter seemed a novelty these days, but it had felt so much better than crying.

He was eyeing her oddly when she met his gaze. "I told you, you have nothing to fear. Not anymore. I shall make sure you are both safe and well cared for."

She stared at him with wide eyes, struck anew by the sincerity in his eyes, at the kindness of his offer. This man who resided in a world of balls and luxury, soirees and debutantes...what on earth had she done to deserve this sort of concern and generosity from a gentleman like him? Here in the firelight, he seemed too good to be true. Larger than life and more handsome than anyone she'd ever met.

For a moment, she wondered if her imagination had conjured him, or if, perhaps, she'd never woken at all from her fainting spell on the steps. "Perhaps I *am* still dreaming," she murmured.

His brows arched. "Pardon me?"

She gave her head a shake and squeezed her eyes shut. "Sorry, it is just...you owe me nothing. I am not your obligation. I don't...that is..." She sighed with impatience at her own stumbling attempts to speak. "I appreciate your generosity, my lord, but I do not understand it."

He tilted his head to the side. "I am a man of honor. As a gentleman, it is my duty to look after those less fortunate."

Charity. That was what he meant. She swallowed down her distaste. After all, someone in her position could not afford pride. And this man, despite his growls and his commands—he'd been nothing but good to her.

And Reggie.

"I suspect perhaps it's more than just honor," she said softly.

His brows drew down. If she did not know better, she would have found that glower fearsome. But she did know better. She'd seen that warmth in his eyes and her dratted mind wouldn't let her forget it.

"What is that supposed to mean?" he asked warily. "If you are worried that I have ulterior motives—"

"Oh no," she hurried to interrupt. "I merely meant that I believe it's your kind heart that has you taking pity on me and my..." She swallowed. "My child."

Now that she'd claimed him as such, she realized how much easier that was to explain. It was safer, too. If word got back to Duncan or any of their acquaintances about a runaway young lady with a little brother, it would be too easy for him to piece it together.

But a young lady and her child that was born out of wedlock?

She was just another cautionary tale.

She could live with that—if it meant that Reggie was safe.

To her surprise, Tolston dropped his gaze to the amber liquid as he swirled it. He seemed discomfited by her comment. "Do not go painting me as some white knight," he said, so low she could barely hear him. "It was not kindness that made me act. Just duty."

She shrugged, bemused by his inability to accept his own goodness. "Perhaps the two are sometimes one in the same."

His scowl made her want to laugh. For the first time in weeks—no, months—maybe even *years*, she felt the urge to tease, like she would have with her father or one of her friends back home. Leaning forward, she met his gaze with laughter in her eyes. "Tell me, do you believe in angels?"

He widened his eyes and then let out a huff of laughter once he realized she was in jest. "No one in her right mind would call me an angel."

She grinned, motioning to her surroundings. "Do I strike you as someone in her right mind?"

She'd meant it as a joke, but his smile faded. "You strike me as someone quite desperate."

"Desperate," she repeated under her breath, her own smile fading as well. "What an ugly word."

He met her gaze evenly, a challenge.

"But true," she added.

He gave a short nod, as if in appreciation for her speaking the truth.

The truth—ha! This man believed her to be an unwed mother. He had no idea the truth behind her situation...or the danger.

Not that she thought Duncan would pose a danger to Tolston. Even if he managed to inherit her father's title, if Reggie was presumed dead—a baron from the countryside up north held nothing on this powerful Earl. Even a sheltered young lady like herself had heard about the great and powerful Earl of Tolston. His friends were dukes and marquesses. Rumor had it he could have his pick of brides. He had the world at his fingertips.

And yet he was sitting here, with her, hoping that she would tell him her secrets. She could see it in his eyes, the curiosity and the expectations.

She bit her lip as she met his dark gaze in the glow of the firelight. Something about this moment—the late hour, the warmth of the fire, the darkness around them—it made her feel close to him. There was something so intimate about it all.

It made her want to give him what he wanted. To spill her secrets here in the safety of his company. Her heart seemed to take a leap in his direction with an unexpected surge of affection toward this near-stranger. She wanted to please him, to make him *happy*—make him smile.

She could chalk these feelings up to gratitude, no doubt. A sense of indebtedness, nothing more.

Because she *did* owe him. Any other gentleman could have tossed her out and not given her a second thought. But not him. Whether he wished to admit it or not, his actions were kind.

And the least she could do was tell him the truth.

Oh, not the whole truth—but some of it.

And if she were being honest, a part of her wanted to share her plight with someone. Even if she could not share everything, she could relieve herself of some of this burden. "I left home because I feared for Reggie."

His eyes narrowed a bit. "You feared for his safety?"

She nodded, turning to stare into the fire rather than face his intensity. She set the plate and glass aside and fidgeted with the hem of her night rail. "The thing is...I don't know if I was right to leave. Sometimes, late at night, I doubt my actions."

"You think you may have made a mistake in running away?" His voice sounded guarded. Careful.

She hesitated over her words. "I...I was scared."

"Undoubtedly." The murmur was gentle. So kind. Her heart hurt when she looked over at him.

"At the time I felt leaving was my only option."

"And now?"

She bit her lip, her mind replaying everything she'd seen

and heard after Duncan arrived. A cold knot of fear twisted within her. "I'm still afraid of the dangers at home."

He was so still across from her she managed to forget him for a moment as she lost herself to memories. Regrets. Fears. The fire lulled her. When she did look over, she gave a start.

Anger played over his features, and in this glow of the fire he looked positively terrifying. "Perhaps I was too quick to call you an angel." She hoped to tease the rage from his eyes. "In this light, you look rather like a devil."

His fierce expression eased slightly. "I don't like the thought of you being in danger or afraid."

"I don't like it much either," she said with a rueful laugh that helped ease even more of his tension.

He sank back in his seat and took a sip of his drink. "I might not be an angel, but I promise I am not quite a devil, either. You have nothing to fear from me."

She wasn't sure if she believed him. She knew he would not intentionally hurt her, but with every second she spent with him, she felt her draw toward him intensify. The more they spoke, the more she felt as though she knew him—and he her. For a lady who'd been suffering from loneliness, that connection was, indeed, dangerous. She would get hurt, because this connection...it would break.

It would have to.

There was no future in which she was in his life, or he in hers.

"You don't believe me," he said.

"No, no," she said quickly, keeping her voice light to break this overwhelming intimacy. "I was just thinking about what you said. You claim not to be an angel, and I do not know if I can agree." He rolled his eyes heavenward, and she laughed. "I will admit, I never imagined an angel to look like you."

He dropped his gaze to meet hers, and she felt his eyes meet hers with a physical jolt. "And just how do I look?"

He was teasing, just like her. But his teasing was different. It was dangerous.

His tone held a note of flirtatiousness that made her belly flip and her heart flutter. Something filled the air between them that made it difficult to breathe. Something heavy and...delicious.

He leaned forward slowly. "Tell me, Miss Adelaide. How do I look?"

Handsome. Devilishly so. She clamped her mouth shut and dropped her gaze, hoping he could not see her blush in this dim lighting. Her mind scrambled to come up with a response—anything that would break this unbearable, sweet, agonizing tension. "Well, you certainly look nothing like Miss Grayson."

That did it. He fell back in his seat with a short laugh. "I should hope not."

She shrugged, feigning nonchalance even as her heart thudded painfully in her chest. "And Miss Grayson," she said meaningfully. "Now *she* looks like an angel."

Tolston grinned—that wicked lopsided smile that made him look like a pirate rather than an earl. "She does rather resemble an angel, does she not?"

An ugly sensation twisted her gut at his easy agreement. She was ridiculous. There was no call for her to be jealous just because Tolston admired Miss Grayson's appearance. After all, who wouldn't? The woman was a beauty.

Addie brushed imaginary crumbs from her lap and reminded herself for the millionth time that she had no claim on this man, certainly no future with him, and he had no regard for her as anything but an act of charity.

"And is Miss Grayson's character that of an angel as her appearance suggests?" Addie was pleased to discover that her voice sounded normal.

Tolston laughed. "I cannot say I know her well enough to make such a claim one way or another."

She returned his smile, that ugly feeling fading somewhat in the face of his grin.

He leaned forward, resting his elbows on his knees. "I do know that she can be trusted," he said. "She will not throw you out because of a child."

She bit her lip. Admittedly she barely knew the other woman, but she did know society and its expectations. No matter how kindhearted, the school's success could be affected by taking in a fallen woman. The other girls there would need to be considered, not to mention the lady who owned the place.

Her mental tangent came to an abrupt halt as Tolston placed a hand over hers.

Her mind ceased its scattered tangents. The whole earth seemed to stop spinning at the feel of his large, warm, strong hand on hers.

"It might not be forever," he said. "But we will figure the rest out in time. For now, however, you will have a home there."

She blinked rapidly as tears rose up at his gentle tone. "And Reggie?"

He squeezed her hand. "I have no doubt Miss Grayson and I will figure out some solution."

She bit her lip to hold back more tears. "You have a lot of faith in Miss Grayson."

His lips quirked up, and his eyes held such warmth it nearly burnt her to her core. "I suppose I do. Her best friend married mine, you know."

He released her hand, and she finally managed to exhale. "No, I did not know that."

"Mmm," he said. "They'd been engaged their whole lives

but only met last year. It was love at first sight...if you believe in such things."

She smiled at his cynical expression. "And I suppose you do not?"

He shrugged. "Do you?"

She opened her mouth and shut it again. *No.* That was what she ought to have said, but when she went to say it she had a flash of warm brown eyes staring down at her, making her feel like she'd finally found the home she'd lost.

She gave her head a little shake instead of answering. It was clearly the late hour that had her so thoroughly rattled. Normally she had much more sense than this, and far more control over her emotions.

"Miss Grayson and I spent this past year watching our friends make fools of themselves over each other." His eyes were filled with laughter. She didn't even mind that it was over the beautiful Miss Grayson just then, because his genuine amusement—not cynical or snide—it was a thing of beauty in its own right.

"That must have been entertaining," she said.

He shook his head with rueful laughter at the memory. "The two of them are romantics through and through."

"Not you, I suppose?"

"Hardly." He smiled. "And neither is Miss Grayson. Perhaps that's why we get on so well. We're both reasonable, rational, and not ones to be led with our hearts."

Addie couldn't help it. She let out a snort of laughter at that.

He arched a brow in question.

"My apologies, it's just... everything you've done for me seems to have come from the heart. No logic would compel a man to help a stranger."

He frowned. "I do wish you'd stop doing that?"

"Doing what?"

"Making me out to be something I am not."

"Kind?" she teased.

He gave a grunt of exasperation that made her laugh.

"Generous?" she continued, loving the way he shifted uncomfortably at the praise. "Admit it, Lord Tolston. You might be more like your friend than you imagined...the kind of man who lives by the compass of his heart."

"The *compass of his heart?*" Now it was his turn to tease, and she loved it. His expression was filled with amusement and disbelief. "Did you really just say that?"

She laughed softly at his disbelief. For the first time in ages, she felt a smile spread across her face—not rueful or wry, not sad or forced, but one filled with happiness at such a simple thing. Teasing and being teased. Who knew it could feel so very good?

She must have been even lonelier than she'd thought.

"Compass of the heart," he muttered again with feigned disgust. "It seems I've found another hopeless romantic, haven't I?"

She laughed when he arched his brows, prompting her for a response. "Admit it," he said. "You believe in the fairy tales —true love, happily ever afters—all that hogwash."

"I did once," she admitted. Her mind wandered back to her childhood. Back when she and her mother had dreamt of balls, and her debut in society, and yes...perhaps even finding a love match. Now it all felt so far away, like the fairy tales Tolston had mentioned.

"Not anymore?" he asked.

She shook her head with a sad smile. "Not anymore."

He studied her for a moment. "You are too young to be so cynical."

She shrugged that off easily. "Perhaps."

His nostrils flared as a flicker of anger crossed his face. "Whoever took your dreams from you ought to pay."

MAGGIE DALLEN

Her eyes widened in surprise, and then she realized what he must have assumed. "I did not mean it like that," she said. "My heart was never broken by anything other than grief. I merely meant..." She threw her hands out at a loss for the right words. "I merely meant, now I know that love is a luxury few can afford."

He met her gaze evenly, searching for what? She knew not. Finally, he tipped his head in acknowledgement. "On that, we agree."

She shifted, unfolding her feet and leaning toward the warmth of the fire, which put her at eye level with him as he continued to rest his elbows on his knees. They were huddled together so closely like they were about to whisper a secret. Maybe that was what gave her the courage—or the audacity, to blurt out the question that popped into her mind. "Are you not holding out for a love match, then?"

He sat upright with a shocked laugh.

"I'm so sorry," she said quickly. "That is none of my business. It's just that everyone is talking about the fact that you haven't wed yet, and—"

"No need to apologize," he said. "You may ask me what you will. We are hardly strangers by now, wouldn't you agree?"

She bit her lip because she didn't know how to answer. His question made her think, and thinking made reality come back to her with a vengeance. For a little while there she'd forgotten herself, her circumstances, her worries...but now?

Were they strangers? No.

But that hardly made them friends.

"No, my lord," she said quietly as she straightened in her seat, folding her hands primly in her lap. "We are not strangers. But I am still only your maid—"

"You *were* my maid," he interrupted sharply. "Now you are my..."

He trailed off as his gaze met hers and held. She found

herself holding her breath as she waited to see how he would finish. What was she to him?

What could she be?

"My charge," he said with finality. "You, Miss Adelaide, are my charge."

CHAPTER 6

There were few things Alec hated more than uncomfortable furniture that was too delicate to be used. Unfortunately, the school's official visiting room was filled with just that. For the ladies who surrounded him, the furniture looked perfect. A handful of petite, pretty young debutantes smiled at him beguilingly.

Well, not Miss Adelaide. *Addie*, she'd told him to call her the other night, but thinking of her as Miss Addie Adelaide still made him smile even as it frustrated the life out of him that he did not know her true identity.

He could find out.

Gregory was just awaiting word to go see Miss Emmaline Haversham.

So why hadn't Alec sent him to get some answers? He wasn't quite sure of that himself. Possibly because he'd rather hoped Miss Adelaide would come clean with those answers herself. That she might trust him enough to share her secrets.

But in the three days that had passed since he'd left her and Reggie with Miss Grayson, he'd gotten none.

Of course, he'd spent no time alone with her since then,

either. He had seen her, though. Every day. The fact that he now recognized every smiling debutante in the room was mildly embarrassing. The fact that they were so familiar with *him* was even more so.

By all accounts, he was here to see Miss Grayson, as a friend and as one of the patrons of this school. Most of the girls came from wealthy families who could afford to pay a great fee to have their daughters taught by the best. Or, in some cases, he suspected—merely have a safe place to keep the young ladies out of sight and out of mind.

But, as designed by Lord Charmian's kind wife, there were some spots left open for ladies without such funds. He and a few others shared that burden. Miss Grayson, in particular, had felt strongly that they should open their doors to young ladies who were at a disadvantage. Ones who suffered from their parents' scandals, or who came from families whose funds had gone dry, or those who had fallen through the cracks, as she'd put it. The ones who were neither marriageable nor on the shelf, not fit for service but not able to run their own homes either.

It was these ladies who Miss Grayson made a point of helping, which was how he'd known that his friend would never turn Miss Adelaide away.

The child, on the other hand—well, the child was the reason for his visit today.

"All right, ladies," Miss Grayson called out as she entered the room. "I believe Mr. Reynolds is waiting for you all in the ballroom."

He heard the redhead next to him sigh. "I am hopeless with dancing."

Miss Louisa Purchase, he recalled. Second daughter of The Viscount of Torrent. Alec wasn't certain she was talking to him, but he felt someone ought to acknowledge her misery. "I am told anyone can learn."

She pulled a face that made him laugh. "Whoever said that never met me."

He leaned over slightly as the other girls got to their feet, chattering amongst themselves. "Trust me. If I could be taught to dance without embarrassing myself, then anyone can do it."

Her eyes widened in surprise before she laughed. "Addie told me you were nicer than you looked, but I didn't believe it until now."

He sat back in shock. She took it wrong, her face crumbling with apology. "Oh I am sorry. I didn't mean it like that." She clapped a hand over her mouth and mumbled something about being abominably rude.

He waved her apologies aside. "I can promise you, it takes far more than that to offend me." Indeed, he was actually feeling quite...pleased. He found himself fighting a smile as he watched her scurry off to join her friends.

So, Miss Adelaide had been talking about him.

He felt like a fool. He *was* a fool. He couldn't even bring himself to meet Miss Grayson's gaze when they were left alone, with none but the dozing housekeeper as chaperone.

Only a child would be feeling this ridiculously giddy joy over the mere fact that a young lady had spoken well of him. *Nicer than he looked.* That was hardly high praise, now was it?

And yet...what was this feeling that had his lips desperately trying to curve up despite his best efforts to squelch them.

Happiness, plain and simple.

Ugh. He was thoroughly disgusted with himself.

"Are you quite all right, Lord Tolston?" Miss Grayson asked.

He sniffed and finally managed to get a handle on his errant smile. Was he all right? No. And he hadn't been ever since a certain young lady swooned in his arms. A young lady who'd been determinedly avoiding any private conversations with him ever since he'd left her at this school.

Easy to do, certainly. Private encounters with eligible gentlemen was hardly encouraged at this school for young ladies, but even so...he knew Miss Adelaide well enough to know that if she'd wanted to speak with him, she would have.

And she hadn't.

Each day she'd been the first one out the door when his visits had come to an end. Today she hadn't even shown up with the other young ladies.

"Where is she?" he asked Miss Grayson now, skipping any niceties because with a friend like Miss Grayson, they were hardly necessary.

As if to prove his point, she merely smiled in response to his abrupt question. "Miss Adelaide, you mean?"

He gave a grunt in lieu of a yes. Miss Grayson was toying with him, albeit in the most subtle manner.

Anyone who did not know the beautiful Miss Grayson would probably not even know she was having fun at his expense.

"She is with Reggie," Miss Grayson said. "The poor boy was sick last night, and she stayed up with him all night."

He came to his feet. "Where are they?"

Miss Grayson's brows arched. "You do not honestly believe I'd let you go to the ladies' private quarters, now do you, Lord Tolston?"

He glared at her, his heart racing uncomfortably at the thought of Miss Adelaide in distress. Even odder, he found he hated the thought of the boy being ill. It was ridiculous. He barely knew the child. But the boy was important to Miss Adelaide. He was a part of her...

And somehow, she had become incredibly important to Alec.

He'd been telling Gregory, Miss Grayson, and anyone else

who would listen that his keen interest in Miss Adelaide and her child was solely born out of obligation. She'd been in his employment, after all. He'd helped her when she'd fallen ill. Surely it was his duty to look after her. Her happiness fell under his concerns.

That was what he said. But he was starting to suspect that this desire to see to her welfare went beyond duty and obligation.

"I wish to see her," he said, doing his best to remain calm and collected...something that had never been an issue for him before Miss Adelaide had come along.

Miss Grayson eyed him oddly. "I'll have one of the girls fetch her."

"Leave her be if she is resting," he said, but Miss Grayson had already slipped out and returned with a small smile. "Your ward shall be here shortly."

Your ward. He cringed at the words. By the way Miss Grayson pressed her lips together to smother a smile, he suspected she knew it. Addie wasn't his ward, she was merely his...his...

Oh blast if he knew what she was to him anymore.

She was his responsibility, that much he knew for certain. But she was also becoming so much more. Something dangerously more.

Miss Grayson sank gracefully into the seat across from his. "To what do we owe the honor of your visit today, my lord?"

Oh yes, she was teasing him. It was rather odd that he'd come to visit so often, that he could not deny.

He toyed with the saucer in his hands, the cup long since emptied of its contents. "I wanted to check on the situation with the boy."

"Reggie?" she asked, as if there was another orphan boy taking up residence here. "I'm afraid I have not had a chance to speak with Lady Charmian yet." Her expression called him a fool so eloquently, there was no need for words.

She'd avoided saying anything to Miss Adelaide—they'd agreed it would do no one any good to get her hopes up—but they hoped that Lady Charmian would agree to allow Reggie to stay on here until he was old enough to be sent to a boarding school.

Alec had already offered to foot the bill for the child's schooling when the time came, and by that point Miss Adelaide would have been at the School of Charm long enough to learn all the skills necessary to gain employment. They might not know who her family was, but if her parents were deceased and there was no one searching for her to claim her... He and Miss Grayson were both of the mind that they allow her the chance to start again here at the school.

With the backing of himself and Lady Charmian, she might be able to find a position as a companion or even a governess or—

"Have you discussed the other option with her?" Miss Grayson's voice was gentle and filled with compassion as they shared a silent exchange. She meant options for Reggie. Whether she might be swayed to part with him so she might find a life for herself.

No one who'd seen Miss Adelaide with her boy would think that she'd be willing to part with the boy. It was clear that she'd go to any lengths to keep Reggie at her side. But anyone with an ounce of sense knew that her options would forever be severely limited should she opt to keep him.

"That was what I was hoping to discuss with her today," he said.

Miss Grayson nodded as the door opened and Addie entered, her head tucked down as she avoided his gaze.

"Then I shall leave you to it." Miss Grayson nodded

toward the elderly housekeeper. "Mrs. Brown shall keep you company."

The old lady gave a loud snore to emphasize the point.

Miss Grayson touched Miss Adelaide's shoulder on her way out and then...they were alone.

Well, alone aside from a sleeping chaperone.

Miss Adelaide dipped into a curtsy, holding the edges of a dark blue gown that did not fit her well since it was borrowed, but still a vast improvement from that brown shroud. "Good afternoon, Lord Tolston," she murmured.

"How is Reggie?"

She lifted her head, her brows rising in surprise. "Better. Thank you for your concern."

He moved toward her, noting how she stiffened. Was she nervous around him? Perhaps their conversation the other night had been too intimate. Definitely far too improper. And yet, he had never touched her.

So how was it that he felt closer to this woman than to any former lover? Whatever had transpired between them in the dark of night made him feel more beholden to her, more connected to her...

And yet, she'd done nothing but keep her distance ever since.

He looked down at the ground. Rightfully so. She had no place in his life. He was on the hunt for a countess, everyone knew that. And no one was less fitting than a fallen woman with an illegitimate child.

Not to mention the fact that he still did not know her name.

She had not trusted him enough to tell him.

Her hands clenched at her sides, and he waited patiently for her to speak. She was summoning her courage to say something, and he'd be damned if he let his impatience get the better of him.

"What will happen to him?" she finally blurted out.

"Miss Adelaide, I—"

"Addie, please," she said with a quick shake of her head. "Please let us be friends and speak plainly."

He hated the desperation in her voice. "What has Miss Grayson told you?"

She bit her lip with another shake of her head. "Only that I need to be patient. That I ought to trust her and Lady Charmian, but..." She sighed wearily. "How am I to do that? Miss Grayson has been so very kind to me, especially given the circumstances. But she barely knows me, and Lady Charmian has never even met me. I have no reason to trust them, nor they me."

The words seemed to come out in a tumble, and he couldn't stop himself from rushing forward to comfort her. Pulling her into his arms, even as he told himself this was wrong. So very wrong.

And yet when she collapsed against him, her head resting against his chest—nothing had ever felt so right.

"You can trust them," he said quietly, his breath rustling the fine hair. This close he could smell her scent, so warm and inviting. He could feel her small frame against his, and the way she fit felt like heaven on earth. Like she'd been made to press against him, to be his comfort, and he her support.

He brushed his lips against her hair, telling himself all the while that he ought to let her go. That this was unseemly and ungentlemanly, and yet he could not stop himself from holding her tight. She shivered a bit against him, but she didn't pull away. She tilted her head back so those sparkling blue eyes were fixed on him. "I don't know who to trust."

"But you trust me," he said. It came out on a low growl, some primitive instinct needing to hear her say it.

"Yes," she whispered. "I trust you."

"Then come to the ball I'm hosting."

Her eyes widened, and she stumbled back a step. "Pardon me?"

He drew in a deep breath, steeling himself for what he had to say. What he'd come here to say. "Are you familiar with Lady Rothby?"

She blinked. "The Viscount of Rothby's wife?"

He nodded and she shook her head no.

"She's a patroness of St. Anthony's," he said slowly, keeping his voice low, gentle. "It's a school—"

"It's an orphanage." Her face had gone pale, her lips thinning into a straight line.

"Yes," he said. "It's an orphanage. Lady Rothby takes great pride in their—"

"No." Her eyes snapped with anger as she tilted her chin up with pride. "I will not give up Reggie."

He did not try to fight her. He couldn't have argued in the face of her firm conviction even though he'd told himself time and again on the way over here that this would be for the best. He had a list of reasons why she ought to at least consider adoption.

Marriage was one of them. She might have a chance of marrying and starting a new family one day if she were to renounce the illegitimate child. Not a marriage to a gentleman, perhaps, but he was certain that with her youth and beauty, she could find a good match with an upstanding man.

The thought was no more tolerable now than when he'd said the same to Gregory over supper last night. His cousin had stared at him nonplussed over his roast as Alec had given a fine speech about the myriad of life choices that would open for Miss Adelaide should she heed his wisdom.

Even then the words had rung false—they'd tasted like charcoal in his mouth—but he'd ignored the ache they'd caused in his chest.

Now, standing here before her, he could barely maintain

eye contact. His mind rattled off reasons why this would be best, but those reasons seemed to wither beneath her fierce glare.

Her eyes sparked with lightning. "I am certain you mean well, Lord Tolston, but I will not be parted from my...my son." She seemed to stumble over the words but her chin tilted up even higher. "I will leave here, if necessary, but I will not—"

"Now wait just a moment," he said, holding his hands out to calm her. "Do not even think of running away merely because I suggested you consider all your options."

She glared at him, and he had to fight a surge of amusement at the wicked glimmer in her eyes. He loved her stubborn streak beyond reason, and the fact that she could stand up to him even when he towered over her with a fierce glower of his own made his heart trip over itself as it tried to race away from him.

Before he knew what he was doing, he'd reached for her hands. She wore gloves this time, but the heat of her still warmed him. Her eyes widened as he squeezed her hands and tugged her closer. "I need you to trust me just a little while longer," he said. He swallowed the urge to beg her not to run. "Please, do not do anything rash. No one will ever force you to give up your son, but it could not do any harm to at least explore your options, now could it?"

Her brows drew down, but she kept her mouth pinched shut.

"As your..." He struggled to find the right word. "As your friend, I owe it to you to give you every choice."

She stared at him for a second, and then her shoulders seemed to slump in defeat. "You owe me nothing," she murmured on a sigh.

He ignored that. He might not be indebted to her, but he still needed to help her. At some point this had gone beyond duty and above obligation, and while he could not explain it even to himself...he knew there was no way he could walk away from her.

No way he could give her up.

He shook off the thought. She was not his for the keeping, but she was his to protect. As was Reggie. The thought of the little boy made him shift uncomfortably beneath her stare. Who was to say this wasn't what was best for Reggie as well?

"Please," he said, startling them both with the plea. "Please just join the other young ladies at my home, and I will introduce you to Lady Rothby. They have all been invited." When she hesitated, he added, "It will be a masquerade." He tried for levity in his tone. "I hear they are all the rage these days. Please come."

She shook her head so quickly he could feel her sudden panic. "No, I cannot. That is, I could never—"

"No one will force you," he said again, his tone as soothing as he could manage. "What could it hurt to hear her out?" He forced a small smile. "Besides, don't all young ladies wish to attend a ball? Do not tell me you aren't tempted..."

He'd managed to tease a reluctant smile from her as she rolled her eyes heavenward. "Of all the matters on my mind these days, ball gowns and waltzes are not exactly a priority."

"No, but perhaps they ought to be." He murmured that under his breath and then caught her eye. It was the truth, and they both knew it. He did not know her family or from where she hailed, but the more he knew her, the more obvious it became that she came from gentility. Standing here in a gown, her hair curled and pinned, her words soft and cultured...there was no mistaking her upbringing. There was only the question now of how no one had noticed it earlier. How had everyone not seen that his maid was a well-bred lady in disguise?

"I cannot live without him," she said. "He is the reason I left, the reason I gave it all up, I cannot—"

"I know." He moved closer and gripped her arms. "Come anyway."

She blinked up at him in confusion, and he could hardly doubt her. He barely understood what he was saying himself. All he knew was that he wanted her there. In his house. On his arm.

He...he *missed* her.

Ridiculous, really. They barely knew one another. And yet, after that evening sitting by the fire, he felt as though he knew her better than most. And when she looked at him— when her gaze met his so direct and unwavering—he got the feeling that she knew him better than anyone else in the world.

"But—"

"Everyone will be there," he said. "You will be surrounded by friends, and I promise no one will force you to do anything you do not wish."

She bit her lip. "Why...that is...why is it important to you that I be there?"

I don't know. He leaned forward. "Haven't you realized by now that I care about you?"

She blinked rapidly, her lips parting for air. His brain grew hazy with desire as he watched her brilliant eyes darken with emotion, her lips so inviting he bit back a groan.

"You...care?" she repeated. She sounded just as dazed as he felt.

He swallowed thickly. He'd said too much, but he couldn't bring himself to take it back. There was something here between them, and he knew that she felt it too. Something that called to him and made him forget about his duty to his title, about the bride he was supposed to be on the hunt for, about the life he was meant to live.

None of that seemed to matter right here and now. Not when she was gazing up at him like this. "Do you trust me, Addie?"

Her gaze softened to something infinitely tender when he used her nickname. She licked her lips, and he tried not to stare. "I already told you that I do."

She sounded just as awed by the fact as he felt.

"Then come to the ball," he said. "Trust that I would not lead you astray."

She hesitated only briefly before nodding. "All right."

Triumph slashed through him, quick and ridiculous. He felt for all the world like he'd won a battle to the death. Her trust in him was humbling, and he found that he was more proud that he'd earned her trust than he was of anything else in his life.

"I will not let you down," he said.

Her lips quirked up in a sad little smile. "You do not know what you promise."

"Perhaps that's because you will not tell me..." He trailed off, arching his brows in question. She gave a quick shake of her head.

No. Despite her trusting him to have her best interests at heart, she did not trust him enough to tell him her secrets.

But that would change. He swore to himself, that would change. "I cannot protect you if you do not tell me the truth."

She bit her lip as she studied him. "I wish I could tell you everything. I truly do." To his horror, tears brimmed her eyes, making them glimmer.

"Don't cry, Addie. We will figure this out."

"No," she said with a sniff. "*I* will figure this out. I appreciate all you have done, but I no longer fit into your world. I have no business being at your home and certainly not attending a ball where everyone knows you are to find a wife."

He gave a start at that. He supposed everyone did know it, but he'd never thought about the fact that Addie knew it.

He hated that she knew it. He felt an uncomfortable sensation—something like guilt—as he met her gaze. It was a struggle not to shift beneath her stare. For the life of him, he did not know whether he felt as though he were betraying his future wife by standing here so close to Addie, or whether he was betraying Addie by searching for his future wife.

Neither made any sense at all, and yet he could not deny that it was guilt he felt right now under her watchful stare.

She took a step back and then another. "I appreciate your help, Lord Tolston. But from here on out, I will decide what is best for me and for Reggie."

She went to walk away, and he could not stop himself. He reached for her, snagging her around the waist and pulling her up against him. He caught sight of her eyes widening, but he was overcome with the need to show her how he felt, to see if she truly felt the same.

He kissed her.

Her lips were soft and warm beneath his, so perfect he thought he might lose all control. He held himself rigid, his grip on her loose enough that she could back away.

She didn't.

They stood there frozen, his lips covering hers in a kiss that was light—almost chaste—as he waited for her to respond.

When she did, it was as though everything in her caved to temptation. One moment she was holding herself rigid, and the next she was sinking into him with a little moan, her arms twining around his neck as he crushed her to him.

He brushed his lips over hers as she sighed. He knew logically that she was no innocent—she'd had a child, after all. But nothing about her response felt studied or experienced as she opened to him.

He should stop this. He knew he should stop. But nothing in the world could have made him. Her lips were intoxicating, the feel of her in his arms like something out of a dream, and the taste of her was better than any nectar.

For one brilliant, heart-achingly perfect moment, Alec felt like he was exactly where he ought to be. He was where he belonged.

He was home.

A snore cut through the moment, and Addie flew out of his arms, backing away until she hit the door with her back, the sound of the housekeeper's snores dwindling once more into background noise.

Breathing heavily, they stared at one another from across the room.

"That...that should not have happened," she breathed.

No. It shouldn't have. But he still hated her saying so. "My apologies, I—"

"No, do not apologize," she said. Her voice was still breathless and flustered as she turned away from him. "I must go."

"Addie, wait—"

His shout roused the housekeeper who sat up straight with a snort. "What is going on?" she demanded.

"Nothing," he said, staring at the door where Addie fled. "There is nothing going on here."

He was telling himself more than her, because it needed to be said. He had to get it through is head.

Nothing should have transpired between them and now... nothing ever would.

CHAPTER 7

As it turned out, Reggie fit into the School of Charm better than Addie did.

At least, that was how it felt some days when she was tired of keeping secrets. Today was one of those days.

Louisa was playing with Reggie on the floor of the dining room long after the other girls had departed. Louisa seemed to love little ones—particularly Reggie. He seemed to take to her brand of open, flirtatious charm just as much as a grown man. He was drooling over Louisa as she beamed at him, cooing her praise when he snatched up the ball she'd rolled his way.

Granted, he drooled quite a bit these days now that the last of his teeth were coming in. But even so, Addie wasn't certain Reggie had ever looked at anyone but her with such adoration.

"I do believe you have an admirer, Louisa," she said.

Louisa flashed her a smile over her shoulder. "If only all gentlemen were so easy to win over."

Addie laughed, as she knew she was supposed to for no one could believe that the brilliantly beautiful Louisa had an issue winning over a gentleman. Addie had heard the tales about Louisa. The other girls at this school might not have welcomed her with open arms, but they were more than happy to inform her of the household gossip. And that gossip?

Well, it seemed to indicate that Louisa had no problem attracting the opposite sex.

But as Louisa had been nothing but kind to her since her arrival, and had avoided discussing Addie's gossip—the least she could do was give her the same respect.

Louisa sat back on her heels as Addie took one last bite of her pastry with a sigh. She would miss the food when she left this place. She'd miss Louisa, too, and Miss Grayson with her calm air and her kind smiles.

She'd miss the dance instructor, whose lessons made her feel like she was a young debutante once more, and the hours of reading aloud in the evenings, which was so cozy and calming and...well, *homey*.

Even Reggie was welcomed to the evening affairs, and it was during those times most of all that she felt like she might actually have a home here. It wasn't the same as her actual home, of course, but here she did not have the specter of Duncan hovering over her, or the bittersweet memories of her parents which made it impossible to forget her grief.

"Are you certain you do not wish to come with us this evening?" Louisa asked.

Addie came back to reality with a start. This evening—the evening she'd been trying not to think about for days. Just like she'd been trying not to think about tonight's host or the way he'd kissed her...

Needless to say, she'd been failing hopelessly on all accounts.

"My blue gown would be stunning on you," Louisa continued.

Addie smiled. "Thank you, but I do not belong there. I'd only stir up more gossip and—" She cut herself short. How to explain that while she'd likely not be recognized by the elite of London, particularly with a mask, there was the chance that Duncan or one of his friends who'd visited would be, and that was a chance she could not take. "It could be a problem."

Louisa seemed to understand what she was not saying. "You might see people you know, you mean," she said, cutting to the chase as she was wont to do.

No one would call Louisa Purchase subtle, that much was certain. But, she hadn't a devious bone in her body, either, and so Addie merely sighed. "That is what I mean, yes."

Louisa tilted her head to the side as Reggie clambered into her lap. "The mysterious Miss Adelaide," she said in a soft sing-song voice. "It is no wonder Lord Tolston is so taken with you, now is it?"

She blinked rapidly. "What? He isn't taken. Why would you say that?" Her voice rose as she spoke, and her cheeks turned hot under Louisa's amused stare. Guilt and embarrassment had her biting her lip before she could babble any more as images of that kiss scorched her brain and made her heart race into action.

"Because I have eyes," Louisa said matter-of-factly. "And ears."

The heat in her cheeks grew so painful, Addie clapped her palms over her face to cool them. Had she heard them the other day?

Oh sweet mercy. Now all she could think about were his groans, her own whimpers—from there it was a slippery slope. She was bombarded by the memory of his touch, his scent, the warmth of his arms around her, and the solidity of his body against hers.

"My, my," Louisa murmured. "I merely meant that he

seems to fuss over you when he comes to visit." She tilted her head to the side. "Is there something more that I'm missing?"

"N-no, no. Of course not."

Louisa's smirk was filled with disbelief, but she did not argue the point. Wrapping her arms around Reggie as though it were second nature to cuddle a small child, she rested her head against the top of his head. "I suppose it's only natural that he take an interest in you since you are his ward."

"I am not his ward." She stiffened in discomfort at the mere thought.

"What would you call him then?" Louisa asked mildly.

Addie opened her mouth and then clamped it shut again. It hardly mattered what she thought of him or how she would classify their rather bizarre relationship. And yet, Louisa was waiting, and his words came back to her, making her warm all the way through. "Friends," she said quietly. "We are merely friends."

"Mmhmm." Louisa sniffed. "Well, I wish I had more friends like the Earl of Tolston, I will say that much."

Addie let out a little huff of laughter at Louisa's teasing.

"But if he is such a dear *friend*," Louisa said. "Then why will you not join us this evening? It really ought to be the most entertaining event." Her eyes grew wide with excitement and her voice breathless with eagerness.

Addie knew that Louisa was rarely allowed to attend society events. She couldn't blame her for being excited— were she in any other circumstances, she'd be eagerly preparing right this minute. But then again, under any other circumstances...she would never have been invited.

Addie studied her friend. "Does your family know you'll be in attendance?"

Louisa shifted, her gaze sliding away guiltily. "Of course."

"Louisa," she said slowly.

Louisa huffed. "It is a masquerade. Who will even notice?"

Addie bit her lip, her allegiance torn between her new friend and the lady who'd been so kind to her. "Does Miss Grayson know?"

Louisa rolled her eyes. "She said that as Lord Tolston invited all of us, I was technically included in the invite. She left the decision up to me."

Addie nodded. "And you don't believe it will cause trouble for her or this school if you should attend?"

Louisa frowned. "Of course not! Addie, I know what you must have heard, but I promise you I do not mean to cause trouble—"

"Of course not, dear." Addie patted her arm soothingly.

Louisa sank back in her seat, slightly mollified. "Trouble just seems to find me, that is all."

"Of course," Addie repeated, this time with a stifled smile.

"But it would help if you were there, too," Louisa said.

"So I can cause trouble?" she teased.

Louisa laughed. "No, silly, so you can make sure I stay away from temptation."

"And what about this evening will tempt you?"

Louisa sighed, but this one was a happy sigh. "Flirting and laughing and dancing..." She gave an exaggerated shudder. "Just think of all the fun to be had."

Addie smiled, and for a second she allowed herself to imagine what life would have been like if everything had been different. If she hadn't gone into mourning before she could have her debut. If her parents were still here to guide her way into society. If Duncan hadn't been named their guardian. If she hadn't felt compelled to flee...

She let out a loud exhale. "I'm certain it will be most entertaining."

"Then come." Louisa leaned forward and squeezed her arm. "Please. For me."

She was about to say no again, but they were interrupted

by the butler who carried a message on a tray. "For you, miss," he said, handing it to Addie.

She opened it eagerly. It would be from Emmaline. They'd been exchanging notes for days as Addie tried to come up with a plan for where she would go from here. She'd be the first to admit...she didn't wish to run. Not again. She'd found a place for herself here, and even Reggie seemed to be content.

But for how long?

She knew Tolston hadn't been trying to hurt her the other day. He'd likely been trying to help. And Miss Grayson, too. But their nudging to have her meet with the Lady Rothby was just another reminder that this situation was not permanent. It might feel like her home now, but it was only temporary.

Emmaline was trying to convince her to talk to her parents, but Addie wasn't sure she could take that chance. She'd never known the Havershams all that well, and had only been friends with Emmaline because of their closeness in age the one time the Havershams had visited their home. All she knew for certain about Emmaline's parents was that they were friendly with Duncan, that much she knew, and it was her word versus his.

Addie read the missive quickly and then read it again in disbelief. *Go to the Tolston ball*, it read. *I have what you need and D. will not be there. He's in town but has other plans. His wards are still at home.*

Addie blinked down at the note. They'd taken to writing vaguely, in case anyone intercepted their letters, but there was still no mistaking her meaning. Duncan was in London, and he'd told the Havershams that she and Reggie were still at their country home.

If she'd had any doubt, it was gone. Duncan had not told a soul they'd gone.

It was not difficult to guess why. Duncan would wait until he believed them to be gone for good and then declare her brother dead. Her too, no doubt.

She supposed she should be glad. Being declared dead was a far sight better than being dead, after all.

And yet, her mouth tasted like grit and dust as she tried to swallow this news.

He would win.

Duncan would get her family home, the money that rightfully belonged to her and Reggie, and they would lose their family and connections to boot.

It wasn't fair. Not even remotely.

The injustice of it made her shake.

But what was she to do?

She studied the note again and again as Louisa entertained Reggie, seeming to understand that she needed silence to think.

Emmaline had the money she needed to run away again and start anew, and the ball tonight was the perfect meeting location. Emmaline would not be questioned about why she was visiting a finishing school on the other end of town, and Addie would not have to risk being seen in the Haversham home.

She wouldn't need to be seen at all at the masquerade—that was the point of these things, was it not?

With shaky hands she set down the note, indecision replaced with resignation. There was no question now about what she ought to do. The answer was right there in front of her in black ink.

Go to the Tolston ball.

That was precisely what she would do.

Once she told Louisa of her decision, Addie's world burst into a flurry of activity. Louisa was in action before she'd finished speaking, with Reggie in tow and three other young ladies clamoring into Louisa's private quarters once they heard the news.

Not all of them were there to cheer her on. She heard one particularly unpleasant girl—a Miss Delilah Olson complaining to anyone who would listen about how unseemly it was for a fallen woman to attend a ball alongside such fine young ladies. Delilah had similar opinions about Addie's attendance at the School of Charm. She made those opinions clear as well, but her friend—the kinder but far more condescending Miss Prudence was quick to point out that Addie was an act of *charity*. Oh, how Prudence seemed to love that miserable word.

She was also certain to loudly laud Miss Grayson's kind and charitable heart in taking in such a *desperate* case as Addie. Prudence said this well within Miss Grayson's hearing, of course, and Addie had once caught Miss Grayson rolling her eyes as she turned away.

Truth be told, that little roll of her eyes had endeared Miss Grayson to Addie more than any kind smile or act of charity could ever have done.

Now, it seemed that despite their disapproval, neither Delilah nor Prudence wanted to be left out of this monumental moment when the notorious fallen lady was to be dressed up for a ball where she hoped not to be seen.

"Why go at all if not to be seen?" Delilah asked. Her long dark hair shone like a mirror, but she continued with her long strokes as a maid bustled about, preparing her gown and hair pins.

They had hours yet until they would leave, but preparations for a ball like this were all-consuming. Most of these young ladies lived for moments like this. If things were different...

Her traitorous mind called up an image of Tolston. Now that she knew how it felt to be in his arms, to be held there like she belonged, like she'd come home—it was all too easy to imagine dancing in his arms. Her entire body felt like it had been swept away by a current of emotion as she braced herself against the delicious thought.

She'd left that life and those dreams when she'd left home.

As if to prove the point, Reggie tugged at the hem of her simple gown, and she leaned down to scoop him up into her arms. She pressed her nose into his white blond hair and held him close until his warmth eased the ache inside her. That hole in her chest that reeked of loneliness and despair. She let his soft comfort and his adorable voice ease the fear that seemed to have taken up permanent residence in her limbs and her heart.

It weighed on her. But no more. If Emmaline could get the funds she'd tried to obtain, then there was a chance that she and Reggie could get away—for good this time. They'd have enough money for a fresh start, one with new names and new friends and—

"Try this one first." Louisa thrust a brilliant green gown in her direction. "This ought to fit perfectly."

Addie took it from her, but she eyed it warily. "Do you have anything a little less...noticeable?"

Louisa tossed her head back with a laugh. "Me? I doubt it. But come along, let us have a look, shall we?"

Addie forced a smile and headed over to the selection of gowns Louisa's maid had laid out on the bed. "Are you certain you do not mind?"

Louisa made a scoffing noise before she was finished speaking. "You, my darling little secret, are the most fun I've had in ages."

Addie shared a grin with the other girls, who seemed to have forgotten what a stain Addie was on their reputations as they gave in to the whirlwind, innocent fun of preparing for a masquerade.

They finally settled on a silver gown for Addie, which was the most subtle shade they could find amongst Louisa's wardrobe. With a gray and white mask covering most of her face, and her hair done in an elaborate style she'd never worn before, she barely recognized herself when she stole a glance in the mirror. "What do you think?" she asked the others.

Louisa clapped her hands in delight with her own work, and Reggie giggled as he aped her gesture. "It's perfect. No one will ever recognize you."

"It is too bad you let yourself be ruined," Prudence said with a sad sigh. "You would have made a beautiful debutante."

Some of Addie's happiness faded as the other girls fell into an awkward silence that seemed to swell with pity as they regarded the strange girl with loose morals whose entire life had been ruined by an anonymous man.

They weren't too far off, Addie supposed. A man *had* ruined her future, just not in the way they imagined.

But—she steeled herself, straightening her shoulders as she met her gaze in the mirror. She ought to be grateful for where she'd landed. It was not every school for young ladies that would even allow a woman such as her through the door, let alone give her every comfort. She was lucky indeed to have found Miss Grayson, and the elusive Lady Charmian of whom she'd heard so many wonderful things. She was grateful for their acceptance of Reggie, just as she was grateful for Tolston.

She firmly shut down any more fantasies about the dashing Earl. She could be grateful to the man for his kindness without turning it into something more. Her life did not include him, and his most certainly did not include her. Or Reggie.

For a moment a whole new temptation called to her. What if she told Tolston everything? What then?

She closed her eyes again and that very possibility swept

through her mind, from the best scenario—he believed her and kept her and Reggie safe—to the worst. He did not believe her and sent her back.

She had a feeling the truth would be somewhere in between.

Perhaps he would believe her, but if she came forward as Miss Adelaide Hopewell, daughter of the Baron of Wrencliff, then Reggie, too, would be once more in Duncan's sights. And so long as Reggie stood between Duncan and the inheritance, he would be in danger.

She couldn't ask Tolston to take on that burden, and she could not trust anyone to care for Reggie as much as she did.

She opened her eyes again, once more ready to face the world. She eyed her reflection warily. Now she knew what she must do. She had to avoid Tolston at all costs. If she were to run away again and give Reggie a life of safety, if not comfort, then she had to steer clear of her biggest weakness, her most devastating temptation.

Tolston.

For while he might have been her strongest ally, he was also the chink in her armor, her Achilles heel. He was the living embodiment of all she was giving up by running away.

He was the future she'd always dreamt about and hadn't even known was real.

He was the future she could never have.

Louisa's arm around her shoulders made Addie sigh with resignation. "You are certain I won't be recognized?" Addie asked again, but this time she wasn't thinking about Duncan's friend or even the Havershams.

She needed to avoid Tolston, at all costs.

"I promise," Louisa said quietly, her voice close to her ear. "He will never recognize you."

CHAPTER 8

Alec recognized her instantly.

He stilled on the second-floor landing that over-looked the main entry, not far from the place where he'd first seen Addie, sprawled out unconscious on his floor. He was mid-conversation with a young lord now as she walked in, flanked on all sides by young ladies who dazzled and stunned with their brilliant gowns and glittering jewels.

Even surrounded by a flock of peacocks, Addie stood out in the crowd.

To him, at least.

It wasn't the gown, or the unique color of her hair. In fact, he would have been hard-pressed to say what it was about her that seemed to call out to him like a beacon amidst all the others.

She might as well have been the only lady in attendance. The others all melted away, paling in comparison next to the light she seemed to emit just by being.

No one emits a light, you fool. He knew it was hogwash, but that did not make him feel any different. Clearly he'd been enchanted by the girl, because she was making his thoughts turn sappy and poetic, and he couldn't focus on anything or anyone for long before she drifted into his thoughts.

He was so far gone that he did not hear his current companion walk away. It wasn't until a female voice wished him good evening that he tore his gaze away from the vision in silver who was still making her way through the crush below.

"I see you've noticed who decided to join us this evening." Miss Grayson's voice was cool and filled with amusement. Not that he could blame her. He would have been equally amused if she were the one standing around like a lovesick fool.

"I thought she was not going to attend," he said, as if that could excuse his humiliating ogling.

Miss Grayson's laughter mocked him, but it wasn't unkind. "I never thought I would see the day."

He tore his gaze away long enough to fix her with a scowl. "I do not know what you mean."

"Do you not?" she teased. "After they way you teased your poor friend Royce for losing his senses so completely—"

"Royce was a fool," he said gruffly. True, Royce was also his best friend, but the two were not mutually exclusive.

"Agreed," Miss Grayson said lightly. "Particularly in trying to keep up pretenses with a woman he so obviously adored."

He shot her a warning look. "If you have a point, Miss Grayson, I suggest you get to it."

She smiled, the effect still stunning despite the fact that a portion of her face was covered with a simple white mask. "Speak to her."

He turned away. "It is not that simple."

"Is it not?" she asked mildly.

"You do not know the situation," he said.

She was silent for a moment. "No," she finally said. "I most definitely do not know Addie's situation." She peeked over at him with a curious look. "And I suspect you do not either."

He huffed in annoyance. She was right, and he hated it. He despised the fact that while Addie might trust him more than some, she did not trust him enough to share her burden and her secrets with him. It grated on him, pricking at his pride and tearing at his heart. "She will not open up to me," he said, the words coming out on a growl of displeasure.

Miss Grayson made a noncommittal sound. "Perhaps that is because it goes both ways."

"What does?"

"Trust," she said. "Vulnerability. *Sharing*."

He gave another growl of distaste at the string of words that rubbed against his masculine sensibilities. But, despite his discomfort—he suspected she was right.

That was the most discomfiting part of all.

"Have you told her how you feel?" she asked.

He snorted in disbelief. "*Tell* her," he repeated. "Tell her what?" He didn't even know how he felt, how was he supposed to tell her?

"I think you know," she said, her tone aggravatingly smug.

He shifted away from her, not sure where he was heading. Though he suspected he'd be wandering the halls of his home until he found her. Addie. She was here, in his home, and there was no way he could stay away from her.

"Have you *told* her?" Miss Grayson persisted.

Now he knew why Lady Charmian had chosen her to run a school. Miss Grayson put every one of his tutors to shame with her persistence and her superior tone, as though she knew the answer as well as him.

And he did know.

Much as he might resist the idea, he knew what she wanted him to admit.

He cared about her. A lot. Too much. Perhaps even enough to call it...love.

He gripped the railing, leaning over slightly to try and catch one last glimpse of her before she disappeared into another room.

"Have you *told* her?" Miss Grayson's tone grew sharper, more insistent.

"No," he muttered.

But he'd *shown* her. That kiss came back to him like it always did these days—insistently and intensely. His body seemed to have a knowledge that his mind and his heart had not yet fully grasped. It was trying to give him a message he didn't entirely wish to hear.

It had spoken to Addie more clearly than his brain and mouth had been able to. That kiss had said all that he could not say.

Miss Grayson shook her head beside him. "I never thought I would see the day," she said again.

He shot her a glare for that all-knowing tone. It was driving him mad.

Even if he could put a name to this strange, new, overwhelming sensation of need and desire and belonging...it did nothing to help him. Even if his heart and body were of one mind, logic, reason, obligation, and duty...they would not be ignored.

Even now, standing here in this crowd of acquaintances and near strangers—this was his home. This was more than his home—it was his family legacy. His title and his land, it was not just his—it belonged to his ancestors and would one day belong to his heirs. There was something humbling about that. It was this knowledge that had kept him from becoming like Royce or any of his other friends, who threw tradition and duty to the wind for the sake of a divertissement and cheap pleasures.

It was that knowledge that made him feel shackled and miserable right now.

He gripped the banister and willed himself to be reasonable. He was a fortunate man in every aspect. The fact that he would be obligated to marry for the betterment of his title was hardly something to weep over. He was lucky. He was blessed.

He was...

He lost sight of her in the crowd.

He was filled with an aching loneliness that made no sense whatsoever. He'd never minded being alone before. Aside from that, he was currently surrounded by hundreds. A close friend even stood at his side.

So why then did he feel like his heart had gone missing the moment she'd left the room? At what point had Miss Addie Adelaide become a necessity in his life on par with food and water?

He wanted her. There was no use denying it any longer. What was more, he needed her. But she was everything he could not have in a wife.

Marrying her would mean scandal, it would mean notoriety and a loss of respect. He would be a laughingstock for being the cuckold who raised another man's child and who married a ruined woman. Not to mention whatever dark family secrets she held that threatened to destroy the both of them if he tied himself to her, to his title...if he made her the mother of his heirs.

But even as he warned himself against it, he found his heart thudding painfully at the thought of her bearing his children, of her at his side, of every night ending in front of the fire—sharing intimacies and hearing her thoughts. Seeing those eyes first thing every morning and hearing her laughter each night before sleep.

As an earl, she was the worst possible choice for a wife.

But as a man?

She was the only choice.

He needed to find her, to speak to her, to make her see sense. Maybe if he could help her with her family problems, if he could save her from her past...maybe there was a chance that they could find a future together.

He turned to Miss Grayson who was watching him calmly, a hint of amusement in her blue eyes in a look he knew well. This was the same kind but cynical gaze he'd seen her turn on Amelia and Royce during the height of their whirlwind love affair.

It was bemusement, amusement, and just a hint of pity for the fool who had lost his mind to the illness called love.

"Has she told you anything?" he asked.

Miss Grayson shook her head. "The girl is tightlipped." She shrugged. "Addie is lovely, sweet, kind, and helpful...but she certainly has her secrets."

"She's afraid of something," he said.

"Yes, that's what's holding *her* back." She turned to face him. "At this particular moment, however, I'm more curious as to *your* excuses for keeping her at arm's length."

He gaped at her. "Is it not obvious?"

She lifted one shoulder. "I never took you to be the kind of man who cared what others thought."

He glared at her mischievous little smile. "And I never took you to be a romantic."

She scoffed and they shared a small smile of understanding. This was one thing they'd always had in common.

"Not for myself, perhaps," she said slowly. "But that doesn't mean I don't believe it exists for others." At his blank stare, she continued on with a defensive tone. "Tell me you weren't just a little swayed watching Amelia and Royce fall head over heels for one another. They proved to me, at least, that love does exist...for some people."

"Not me." He said it more out of habit than anything else, but it was the truth, was it not? Addie had said it herself. Love was a luxury few could afford.

Was that what this was? A luxury? Were he to cave to his wants and desires for this wholly unsuitable woman would he be giving in to selfishness or doing right by himself and, more importantly, by her?

He could end her suffering easily. He might not know her secrets but with the power of his title and the fortune at his disposable, surely her fears could be conquered. There was nothing he would not do to ensure her safety, and the safety of her child.

Was it selfish to want love in addition to everything he'd been given? Perhaps. Maybe it was too much to ask of fate that he have love as well as wealth and power and a good name.

Was that it, then? Was the price of his good fortune a life without true love?

He looked out over the sea of noisy people below. What a depressing thought. To go his whole life without genuine affection and a true connection...for what?

As an earl he had more money than he could count, more power than all but a handful, and more respect than any. No scandal would harm his banknotes, and no amount of notoriety would steal the power of his title.

It was his pride that would take a licking.

But what had all that pride gotten him?

Certainly not warmth or happiness...or love.

He drew in a deep breath and clenched his hands into tight fists. The need to see her right this instant, to tell her how much that kiss had meant to him—it made him want to crawl out of his skin. At the very least, he wanted to leap over this balcony to avoid the mass of people who were crowding the staircase and impeding his path.

These people—he watched them now with a new vision. One of a man in love, he supposed. They might judge her, but *he* knew her worth, even if he never knew her history. And if they judged him a cuckold?

Well, again...he knew better.

So what did he have to risk if he asked her to be his? Only his pride.

But if he didn't pursue her—if he let her slip out of his life the same way she'd come in, he'd lose his heart. Of that he was certain.

"Pardon me, Miss Grayson, I need to attend to some business."

"Give Miss Adelaide my best," she called after him.

"Adelaide." A male voice he did not recognize repeated the name as though it meant something. "Did you say Miss Adelaide?"

But when Alec turned to see who it was he found the crowd had shifted behind him and he found himself facing a crowd of masked gentlemen and ladies who were carrying on with chatter and laughter. He shoved aside the niggling doubt that had stolen over him and headed once more for the staircase.

For once in his life, he was going to act selfishly —impulsively.

For once in his life, he was going to follow his heart.

He could only hope he wasn't too late in telling Addie how he felt, and that he could convince her he was worth taking a chance on. That he was truly worthy of her trust and her faith.

They'd deal with whatever ramifications came together. They'd forget her past and his. They'd build a future of their own—one that included the two of them and Reggie.

Was it unconventional? Perhaps. Would he have to reckon

with her family when they discovered where she'd run off to and why? Undoubtedly.

A new sense of purpose had him striding down the stairs, slipping past groups of partygoers with determined focus.

And if he lost the respect of the *ton*? So be it. It was better than losing his self-respect, and that was what was at stake if he gave up on the lady who'd brought his heart to life and breathed new meaning into his existence.

He reached the ground floor, heedless of the calls for his attention or the looks cast his way.

He was on a mission to find Addie. Once again he was chasing after her...but this time there was one major difference.

This had nothing to do with saving her and everything to do with saving himself.

CHAPTER 9

All she had to do was find Emmaline, then she could leave.

The reassurance did little to settle her nerves. Being here in his house again—it was unnerving. She'd only stayed here a matter of weeks, and while under the guise of a maid, at that.

And yet it still felt like her home, in an odd sort of way. Here she'd been safe, at least for a little while. The grand townhouse felt loaded with memories—too many to fit even into this large home with its high ceilings and wide doorways.

She slipped through one of those doorways now, eager to find a place less crowded where she could peruse the guests and hopefully seek out her cousin.

Emmaline had to be here somewhere. Addie had heard the Haversham name announced not long after her own arrival. She and Emmaline had foolishly not thought to name a meeting spot, and now she was stuck wandering through the party, trying to avoid running into anyone who might recognize her—although that list was admittedly small—and trying her best to avoid Tolston.

That was easy enough to do. Last she'd seen him, he'd been looking down over the crowd like a king on his balcony. That dark, brooding gaze had swept over the crowd and then over her like he could see all of her. Everything the mask hid, right down to the most deeply buried hope and wish.

Stuff and nonsense.

He could not see her heart pounding any more than he could have seen the blush on her cheeks at the mere sight of him. Thank heavens for her mask. With it on she felt almost safe.

Emmaline had assured her that Duncan was not attending tonight, though he was in town.

All was safe.

She hoped.

Though the fact that Duncan was anywhere in this city had her more on edge than ever. The sooner she could get the money and get far away, the better.

At last! A tall blonde woman appeared at the other end of the room, hovering in the doorway as she glanced this way and that.

Addie had no doubt it was Emmaline. Not many women were so tall that they could be seen over the crush even from the other side of the room.

Addie waved a hand, and her cousin started forward toward her before she was stopped by a gentleman who was speaking to her. Addie hovered where she was, afraid of avoiding attention by standing there alone and afraid talk to her cousin lest this gentleman be someone she knew.

She inched forward, slowly but surely making her way over. When she was directly behind the man still talking to her cousin, she stopped short. She could not make out the words but...that voice.

She'd recognize it anywhere. Low, cold, and so terrifying it made her heart race. *Accidents happen all the time to little children*. This was Duncan's friend. The visitor she'd never seen but who had casually suggested murdering her brother.

She stumbled back a step, bumping into a reveler who laughed heartily at something his friend was saying.

All Addie could hear was her own breathing, harsh and far too loud.

What was he doing here?

Who was he?

A part of her wished to move forward and hear what he was saying as another part of her fought the urge to flee. She ended up standing still, frozen in place. Nothing would bring more attention to her than sprinting madly through a crowd.

She watched Emmaline, cursing the elaborate mask that hid her cousin's face. She could not even tell if her cousin was speaking or listening...

Finally, just when she thought she might scream, the tall gentleman with the raven black hair walked away, back out the way he'd come. She lost sight of him when he turned the corner, but she still waited, frozen in fear that he might turn back around and see her.

You're wearing a mask, she reminded herself, hoping that might ease her fears and stop her heart from racing away from her. *Even if he saw you, he would not recognize you.*

She wasn't even certain he knew what she looked like. She hadn't caught sight of him at her family home when Duncan had hosted his friends, but that did not mean *he* had not spotted *her*.

Emmaline was moving toward her and jumped when Addie reached out and snagged her arm. "What did he want?"

"Adelaide!" Emmaline exclaimed.

Addie shushed her and pulled her toward the wall where they might find a modicum of privacy. "Please, Emmaline," she said. "What did that man say to you?"

Emmaline sighed. "After all this time, and with all you've

been through...you want to talk about some stranger?" She clutched her hands, her voice urgent. "Tell me where you've been, how you are. How on earth did you end up at Lady Charmian's school?"

"Emmaline," she said, her impatience growing. "Please. I know you have questions, but that man, he is a friend of Duncan's."

Emmaline rolled her eyes. "Of course he is, dear. You must recall how popular Duncan is. Everyone loves him."

Adelaide gaped at her cousin. True, she had not told her the details, but surely her cousin had not fallen for his charms, knowing as she did that he'd all but driven Addie from her home.

Emmaline eyed her now, as if trying to gauge her sanity—or perhaps that was Addie's paranoia kicking in. "Duncan arrived at our house last night unexpected. He came to pay his respects to Father."

She'd assumed as much, but hearing it still made her stomach twist in fear. "He is not here tonight, though—"

"No," Emmaline said quickly. "Duncan said he had other plans when my mother asked him to join us this evening. But Addie..." Emmaline's eyes were soft with kindness. The two ladies hadn't spent much time together over the years, but Addie remembered their time together as children fondly. Right now, at least she knew she had one true friend in this world.

"What is it?"

Emmaline drew in a deep breath. "Last night...he told my parents that you ran away."

Adelaide held her breath as she waited for more, dread filling her stomach and making the contents there churn with nausea. "Did he say why?" she asked in a small voice.

Emmaline fidgeted uncomfortably. "He...he said you were having episodes."

"*Episodes?*" Her voice held all the disbelief she felt and for a moment she forgot to keep her voice down.

Emmaline bit her lip, looking pained at what she was about to say. "He made it sound as though...as though you had lost your wits," she said on a rush of air. "He said you were overcome with grief and you'd gotten ridiculous ideas in your head and—"

Emmaline cut herself off as Addie gasped in dismay. "He didn't."

"I'm afraid he did."

"Did they...did your parents...did they *believe him?*"

Emmaline's silence was answer enough. A jolt of pain shot through her, a new form of loneliness she never knew existed until now. "Do *you* believe him?" she whispered.

Emmaline still looked pained as she struggled for an answer. "No, of course not," she said after the briefest hesitation. It might have been brief, but it had been telling.

"Emmaline, please, you must believe me."

"I do," she said, more convincingly this time. "It's just that...I wonder if perhaps you misunderstood. Or perhaps he was joking—"

"About murdering my brother?" she snapped.

Emmaline let out a sigh. "No, you're right, of course. I suppose I have a hard time believing anyone could be so cruel."

Addie sighed as well. She could hardly fault her sweet cousin for not wishing to believe the worst in someone— especially someone they both called family.

"He's here to find you...and Reggie," she said.

Addie's heart stopped at the mention of her brother. "He knows we're here?"

Emmaline shrugged. "Perhaps he just assumed you would come here as we're your only living family."

That sense of loneliness? It was painful right now. So few

people to rely on in this world and it seemed most of them believed her to be crazed with grief.

"H-he—" Emmaline stopped short.

"He what?"

"He insinuated that he feared for Reggie's safety. That some harm may have come to him for you to go..."

"Insane?" she offered, her voice rising with incredulity. She was having a hard time fully comprehending what her cousin was saying as a sort of numbness stole over her. "I need to leave."

Reggie was back at the school with only the housekeeper and an old butler as a guardian. What sort of sister was she that she'd left him on his own?

She'd grown too comfortable here in London, she'd deluded herself into thinking she and Reggie were safe with Lord Tolston and Miss Grayson looking after them.

She'd been wrong.

So very wrong.

Her breath started coming too quickly as her pulse raced erratically.

"Emmaline, I must go. Do you have the money?"

"Yes, of course, it's right here." She reached into her reticule and then thought better of it. "Here, take it all."

Clutching the bag to her chest, ready to flee when the memory of that cold black-haired gentleman gave her pause. "That man talking to you just now..."

"Lord Everley?" she asked, her brow furrowing in confusion.

Lord Everley. So, now she had a name with the voice. "Yes," she said. "What was he talking to you about?"

"Duncan," she said easily. "He was looking for him, he said they had much to discuss."

"Did he mention me?" she asked warily.

Emmaline's eyes filled with confusion. "No," she said

slowly. "He just asked me to give Duncan a message in case I saw him before he did."

"What was the message?"

Emmaline frowned as if still confused by it all. "Something about how he'd found the gift he'd been looking for on Devereaux Row but they'd shipped it to the wrong address...?" Her voice trailed off in a question.

The blood drained from Addie's face, her limbs turning to ice as she froze in place. Devereaux Row.

"Maybe I got that wrong, I was so distracted trying to find you I was not terribly attentive, I'm afraid." Her cousin frowned at her. "Are you all right?" When Addie didn't immediately answer, she shifted closer. "Does that mean anything to you?"

Devereaux Row. That was the street where Mrs. Grishny lived. It was where Reggie had been staying right up until Tolston had forced her into attending Miss Grayson's school.

What were the odds that the cruel lord—Lord Everley— was referring to something else?

Slim. Very slim. Oxygen seemed to be in short supply as she took in shallow gulps of air. Her head was spinning, her hands were clammy, and she could have sworn she heard someone calling her name.

"Miss Adelaide!" A voice she knew as well as her own had her stiffening in fear. "Miss Addie Adelaide." There was no mistaking that lazy drawl as his voice cut through the crowd around her.

She widened her eyes as panic sliced through her. She had to run. There was no way she could face Tolston right now, not when she was so vulnerable and terrified. If she spoke to him, he would know something was wrong.

He would know she was about to run.

She couldn't let him stop her. Not this time. She had too

much at stake. Reggie's life depended on her being strong, even if that meant hurting the man she loved.

She squeezed her eyes shut for a moment before bracing herself for what was to come. She opened her eyes to find Emmaline watching her with concern.

"Are you all right?" Emmaline asked, her voice breathless as she looked from Emmaline to Tolston and back again. "Is Lord Tolston coming for *you?*"

Before she could answer or even begin to explain, he was upon them. "Addie, at last I've found you."

It might have sounded sweet and romantic if his tone wasn't so curt. He sounded irritated and annoyed—a fact which might have amused her at any other time. As it was, she couldn't quite bring herself to meet his gaze, which was focused solely on her.

He didn't seem to notice Emmaline or any of the others who gathered around, stealing glances to see what had their famed host moving through the crowd with such urgency.

Addie tried to shrink in on herself as she felt their stares, fidgeting with her mask to better cover her features.

"You came." Tolston growled this like it was an accusation.

"You invited me," she shot back.

He let out an exhale of exasperation and ran a hand through his hair. "I did not mean to—oh blast, let me start over."

She started to back away. He was too close, his proximity was a danger in and of itself. She had to get out of here, and Tolston was too much of a temptation. His heat, his strength, his affection. The way he was looking at her like she was the only person in this room.

He would help her. She knew that. If she told him she and Reggie were in danger, he would help her.

But at what cost?

He would demand everything from her, and she could not give him that. She would need to tell every secret, reveal every lie.

She had no time for that.

And what if he did not believe her? What if she wasted her breath and found out that he too was a friend of Duncan's? What if he believed Duncan's lies over her admittedly ludicrous story?

She couldn't risk it.

She steeled her senses as he moved closer. "We must talk, Addie."

Shaking her head quickly, she moved closer to Emmaline, who'd never budged despite Tolston's rude behavior. Thank heavens for her kind, supportive cousin. She'd never survive a moment alone with Tolston, not when the memory of their kiss was wreaking havoc with her heart just because she could smell his scent. If he were to touch her, speak tenderly to her...

She would never have the strength to do what must be done.

"Do you hear me?" he growled. "I must have a moment alone—"

"There is nothing to say," she interrupted. She could feel Emmaline's gaping stare at his forward words. "We have *nothing* to say," she repeated.

"Maybe you don't, but I do." He moved even closer and her heart raced that much faster. Between her fear and her desire, her body seemed to thrum with energy, her limbs itching to move.

To run.

"I have given this much thought, Miss Adelaide." He lowered his voice so no one else could hear, not even Emmaline. That low growl of his was meant for her, and her alone. Her traitorous body ached to lean forward to hear him better.

She nearly cried from the stab of longing that had her imagining what it would feel like to rest against him now, to cry on his shoulder and allow him to ease her every concern.

The temptation was very nearly too great to deny. "I'm sorry, but I must leave, Lord Tolston. We can talk another time." If she wasn't already gone...

"I want you, Addie."

She blinked once. Twice. Surely her ears were playing tricks on her, his voice was too low that even she was mishearing. "Pardon me?"

"I want you to be my wife." He'd taken off his mask at some point, and there was nothing there to shield her from the intensity in his eyes, the stubborn set of his jaw, the determination that had his features set in stone.

She was shaking her head in disbelief, certain she was hearing things, when he reached out and gripped her upper arm. "Come with me, please," he said.

It was the please that made her know he was serious. He was not the kind of man to beg or even ask permission. "W-why?" It was the best she could manage in her stunned daze.

"Because this is a conversation best held in private," he said. His eyes burned with need and desire and...could it be? Was that *love* she saw there?

She sucked in air, feeling once more like it was doing nothing to help her. She felt dizzy with all the emotions swirling inside her. "Y-you want to marry me?" She shook her head. "But you barely know me—"

"I know how I feel, and that is all I need to know." He moved in so close she had to tilt her head back to see him clearly, the sight of him all encompassing, the sound of his voice turning everything else into a dull roar.

"But I am not...that is, I couldn't be—"

"Why not?" he demanded.

She stared up at him. He could not be serious. But then...

to tease her like this would be cruel, and she couldn't imagine a world in which the great and noble Earl of Tolston was cruel.

"You do not know my family," she started, her voice filled with disbelief as she tried to understand what he was saying.

"I do not need to know them," he said. "I know you."

Her mouth fell open in shock. She was dreaming. That had to be the case. There was nothing else for it. No gentleman—no earl—would offer to marry an unwed mother with no family, at best, and a scandalous one at worst.

He had no idea what he'd be getting himself into.

He might not even believe her if she told him.

"But...Reggie," she started.

"Will live with us." It was the decisiveness in his tone that finally made her come back to reality.

He was serious.

He would wed her and take in Reggie...why? Because he cared about her or out of some misguided notions of obligation and duty?

She took a faltering step sideways, bumping into Emmaline in the process.

"Addie, is he serious?" she whispered, her voice tinged with awe.

Apparently one person in this crowd *had* heard his crazy proposition. And that's what it was. Crazy. Ludicrous. There was no way he wouldn't change his mind once he got over whatever this was between them.

"I cannot," she started, her voice little more than a breath.

"Why not?" He was glaring at her like he had so many times before. So imperious, as though there was no doubt that he would get his way.

He would marry her.

The thought made her heart feel like a hummingbird in

her chest. The very thought was so appealing—to be close to this man always. To share whispers and kisses and...*secrets*.

Her secrets weighed on her chest now like an anchor. Where to begin? How to even start?

Imagining his reaction—his disbelief—it was too much to bear. "I cannot talk about this now," she said.

His brows drew together in confusion. "Come away with me somewhere private."

"I just told you, I cannot." But he didn't seem to hear her.

"If it is Reggie you are concerned about, I can allay your fears."

He continued talking, but she no longer heard him. All she could hear was the buzzing in her ears as her earlier fear returned with a vengeance. Panic and regret vied for authority over her as she realized she'd very nearly forgotten about Reggie in her stunned state.

He was home, alone but for an elderly housekeeper and a butler who was partially deaf. He was vulnerable, and someone might very well know where he was.

If they had tracked him to Mrs. Grishny's, who was to say they hadn't learned of his current hiding spot?

"I have to go." Her voice sounded too high, too airy.

"Addie? What is wrong?" It wasn't so much a question as a demand for answers.

This...this was why she had to escape. He would never let her leave until he knew all and even then he would take matters into his own hands.

She had to act now, and she had to do what was best for Reggie. What was best for them both.

She had to run.

"I—I—" She was tripping over her own feet trying to get around Emmaline, who was helping to keep her upright.

Thank heavens for Emmaline.

"I have to leave," she said. "We will talk later."

They wouldn't. She would be gone, but it seemed the best way to get away. She couldn't deal with the emotions that came with talking alone with Tolston. Not now...maybe not ever.

"Addie, wait—" he started, but for once in her life her small stature worked to her advantage as she slipped under an elbow and between two people standing close together. She wove and wound her way through the room, heedless of manners, her only focus on getting out and getting to Reggie before Duncan or Lord Everley beat her to it.

Behind her she heard her name being called. Tolston. He wanted her, or so he said.

But what if what he wanted was a damsel in distress? A lady to save. When he looked at her, he saw a woman who needed saving. She wanted more with him.

She wanted *everything*, truth be told. She wanted the fairy tale ending she'd always dreamt for herself.

But she'd grown up these last few months. She'd had to. Reggie wouldn't survive on fairytales, but from cunning and strength.

If there was any chance of a life for them, she had to leave behind childish fantasies and outlandish dreams.

She had to leave behind the hope of finding love.

CHAPTER 10

A lec watched her run, darting through the crowd like a murderer was on her tail.

What...what on *earth* had just happened here?

His head was still spinning in disbelief as he turned to her friend. "What just happened?"

The tall lady's apologetic grimace said that she'd heard what he'd said just now. Every word of it, no doubt.

By her wide-eyed stare beneath that mask, he'd guess she was just as shocked by his behavior as he was. He cleared his throat. "My apologies for interrupting your conversation with Miss Adelaide, Miss...Haversham, is it?"

She nodded. "Yes, my lord."

He cleared his throat as he looked around as if someone might come along and salvage this situation. How?

He had no idea.

Perhaps they could provide an introduction to the young lady present whom he'd just shocked into a stupor. That would be a start at restoring his dignity, at least.

The lady in question cleared her throat as well, and he had

to wonder if perhaps passersby thought they were in quarantine together. Two partygoers falling ill at once.

He did feel ill, come to think of it. Deathly so. He stared at the space where Addie had been. He felt like he'd lost a rather vital organ. His heart, to be precise.

"I believe we met at my parents' hunting party in the country last year."

He whipped his head around to face this woman who'd witnessed his heartbreak, and what could also adequately be described as the most humiliating rejection of his life.

But at least he'd made a proper introduction with this young lady...even if he couldn't quite remember it. "Yes, of course," he murmured. Polite civility was so ingrained in him that he found himself saying what he ought to say even when his mind was elsewhere.

It was still trying to sort out what on earth had just happened and how he'd managed to so badly mangle what ought to have been a welcome proposal and a guaranteed acceptance.

"I *am* an earl, am I not?" He wasn't quite sure why he said the word aloud, but there it was. His confusion was beginning to form a voice of its own.

"Indeed, my lord."

He could have sworn he caught a glimmer of amusement in her eyes, along with a hefty dose of pity.

Wonderful. He was being pitied by a too-tall wallflower at his own ball.

"I should, uh..." He looked around, searching for some duty that called. Everything in him wanted to chase after Addie, but a man had his pride.

Granted, he'd done away with most of that pride when he'd proposed to her—here. In public.

Where she'd then refused him.

But being seen chasing her throughout his house like he

was enacting some scene out of a melodrama—that was absolutely beneath him.

And her.

Which begged the question...what had come over her?

For the first time since she'd run, the sharp pain of her rejection and the brutal blow to his ego faded long enough for his brain to function properly. "Why did she run, Miss Haversham?"

He fixed his stare on Miss Haversham, and the poor lady visibly blanched, that much was apparent from the little he could see of her face. His tone was hardly cordial, his question impertinent, and yet...he found he did not care.

Not in the least.

In fact, the more the thought about the look in Addie's eyes before she'd fled—

He knew that look. He'd seen it before. In the moment, he'd confused it with shock over his admittedly abrupt and unexpected proposal. But now....

Now, he wondered.

Shifting closer to Emmaline, he dropped his voice. "Before I arrived, what were you two discussing?"

"I, uh, I..." Now it was her turn to eye the door frantically, as though she too wished to follow in Addie's footsteps.

"Miss Haversham," he started, his tone a warning.

"It is not for me to say, my lord."

He had to admire the fact that her gaze once more met his, but her pert tone was forced. He could see the way she fidgeted with her fan, the way her breathing was shallow like she was fighting all-out panic.

"I have no wish to harm her, Miss Haversham." He kept his voice low and smooth. "I love her."

"Yes," she said, as her gaze darted left and right, seeking help, no doubt. "I gathered as much when you proposed."

He felt a flicker of amusement beneath his fear and his

pain. Perhaps that ill-conceived proposal had its merits after all. There could be no better way to prove his loyalty for Addie than to offer for her hand in marriage.

In front of this lady.

"How, may I ask, did you come to be so close with Miss Adelaide?" he asked.

He never did have Gregory look into this lady and her connection to Addie, and now he regretted it mightily.

"We are relatives...my lord." She tacked on the title belatedly, her demeanor one of distraction as she looked around them. "I...I really cannot tell you more." She bit her lip as she sneaked a look back at his face. "I am sorry. Truly. I know you care about her, but she believes she may be in danger, you see—"

"Danger?" The word made his insides freeze. The wording of it was odd—she *believes* she may be in danger. "Why would she think that?"

She pressed her lips together and gave a little shake of her head. *No more*, that shake said. She'd already said too much.

"Is it her family?" he asked. "Is she worried about what they might do to her if they discover Reggie?"

She pressed her lips together tighter but he caught the flicker of confusion. No. Not her family, then. He moved in closer and she held up her hands in surrender. "Please, Lord Tolston. Do not ask me any more questions. I have already said more than I ought."

"You can trust me, Miss Haversham." *You can trust me, even if Addie does not.* He shook off the thought. He would deal with her later, once he found her and made sure she was safe.

Safe and healthy and *his*, preferably until the end of time.

That wasn't asking too much, now was it?

Miss Haversham seemed to be growing ever more determined to keep her silence by the moment. And when he thought about it, he could not fault her. If Addie were some distant relative who'd run from her home because she was with child, she would hardly spill her secret to just anyone, even if that anyone had offered marriage.

"Miss Haversham, if it helps to ease your fears, I can tell you this—I know about Addie."

"Y-you do?"

He let out an exasperated sigh. No, not entirely. He didn't know her whole story, but he thought he knew enough. At the very least, he was certain he knew Addie's biggest secret and the one which Miss Haversham would be utterly unwilling to share.

He leaned in closer and dropped his voice another octave. "I know about Addie and her *son*."

Miss Haversham's head jerked back in shock. "Her *son*?"

They both looked around quickly, and Miss Haversham clapped a hand over her mouth in obvious horror at having shouted the word to the rooftops.

She'd shouted it in disbelief. Because...because *why*?

His brain still felt stilted and creaky after all the events of this evening. A little part of him was still replaying Addie's rejection and watching her run away from him. But the part that *was* functioning properly—it started to race as pieces clicked into place. "Reggie is not her son," he said.

It was not a question.

Miss Haversham blinked her wide eyes. It was neither confirmation nor protest, but he did not need her to confirm it. He knew it. The truth settled into his gut with a rattling *clank*. After all, Addie had never introduced Reggie as her son —he'd assumed. They all had.

The more he thought about it, the more he realized just how little she *had* told him. How vague she'd been, and how very evasive.

He shifted uncomfortably, tugging at his cravat. He'd been prepared to marry the lady, and he truly knew nothing about her.

But no. That wasn't entirely true, either. He might not know her history, but he knew her heart.

He found himself glaring at a clearly terrified Miss Haversham. "I-I am truly sorry, my lord, but—"

"Enough with the apologies," he said with an imperious wave of his hand. "I need to know where she is. I need to know now."

She blinked rapidly, and for a moment he feared he'd gone too far. He'd meant to be stern with the girl, not make her cry.

"My lord, I made a promise, and—"

"And the fact that you mean to keep it makes you a valuable, loyal friend," he said, gentling his tone. He took a step toward her, all too aware of the eyes that were on him. On *them*. A lifetime spent avoiding gossip and now he seemed to be vying for scandal like it was his duty to provide it.

"But here is the thing, Miss Haversham," he continued quickly, his voice low but urgent. "You care about Addie, as do I. If you heard even a snippet of what just occurred here, you must know how very much I care about her."

She hesitated only briefly before giving a short nod. Hardly a rousing endorsement, but he would take it.

"I care about her too much to see her hurt, as I imagine you do as well," he continued. The very act of trying to remain calm and patient nearly destroyed his sanity. One thing he knew about Addie was that she was strong. Brave. If she could stand up to the likes of him, then she could stand up to anyone.

So, whatever had her running out of here tonight like a ghost was on her tail, it had to be a real threat. Real and frightening.

"Where was she running off to just now, Miss Haversham? I must know."

She bit her lip, confusion and wariness clear in her eyes. While he wanted to shake the girl, he couldn't fault her for wanting to remain loyal.

"If she is in harm's way, I can help her," he said. "But only if I know how to find her."

She gulped visibly, clearly alarmed at the thought of harm coming to her friend.

"Where is she, Miss Haversham? Tell me, and I promise you I will save her and make this right."

As Miss Haversham wavered, he found himself struck by the fact that he was asking a stranger to have faith in him where Addie had not. He was asking this lady to have faith in him when the woman he meant to call wife hadn't even trusted him with the truth.

He shook off the thought and met Miss Haversham's gaze evenly. "Please. I promise to help her."

She closed her eyes briefly. "I do not know for sure where she's gone, but I can tell you this. It was not her own welfare that she fears for, but her brother's."

Her brother.

Reggie.

Alec was already moving toward the exit as he said his thanks and made a rather rash promise to make sure that all would be well for Addie from this moment forward.

Could he swear to such a thing?

Perhaps not.

He had no idea the extent of her troubles, and for that he could kick himself. Why had he not tried harder? Why had he not done his due diligence and checked into her story?

Because he'd been distracted, that was why. For the first time in his life he'd been besotted, and the effect had been to turn him into a blind, lovesick fool.

He hurried into the servants' quarters and had the butler call for his carriage.

He might not be able to save Addie from whatever trouble she was in...but he was certainly willing to die trying.

CHAPTER 11

Addie wasn't fully able to take a deep breath until she'd launched herself into Reggie's room and found him sleeping soundly under his covers.

Only then did she slump against the doorway, a sob of relief welling up in her which she stifled with a hand over her mouth, water dripping down her cheeks from the downpour that had started just as she'd reached the school's front entrance.

She allowed herself three blissful seconds to revel in relief and happiness that Reggie was here, unharmed...and then she moved into action.

Duncan was here. In town, if not at this school. But, if he'd tracked Reggie to Mrs. Grishny's, it was only a matter of time before he found him here.

As quietly as she could, Addie gathered what few belongings they'd had before they'd arrived, neatly setting aside the borrowed gowns and hair pins as she once more donned her traveling frock. The very act felt like stepping backward in time. Gone was the silvery, ethereal silk, and in its place was a rough, worn brown garb that reminded her of all she was leaving behind.

I want you to be my wife.

She stilled in her movements, closing her eyes tightly against the rush of pain.

He'd been serious. Her mind was still trying to wrap itself around that fact. Yes, he'd kissed her, and she'd never doubted that there was a very real connection between them—there had been from the first moment their eyes had met and held.

Back when she'd thought he was a kindly doctor.

Back before he'd taken her life into his hands, and saved her and Reggie, and talked to her like she was an equal.

Back before he'd kissed her.

She drew in a deep, steadying breath, systematically forcing away the sensations and emotions that were making her weak when she needed to be strong, soft when she needed to be hard.

Duncan was here. The man with the cold, hard voice was here. Lord Everley. Not that having a name to the voice did her much good. All it did was confirm that he was a lord, which meant he held even more power than Duncan.

Duncan was here, and he had powerful friends working with him. That was what was important right now. The only thing she could afford to think about. Reggie's safety was more important than her happiness. And Tolston? Well, she had a feeling he was her happiness.

The life he'd offered so unexpectedly and rashly...it sounded like every dream come true. To be wed to a man who looked at her as he did, who cared about her more than he cared about society's expectations, who was a good and honest and dutiful man she could respect and admire.

He was a man she could love.

Her breath came out shaky as tears brimmed her eyes.

He was the man she *did* love.

It was useless to deny it when her heart was breaking at the thought of leaving him.

A noise below stairs had her swiping at her arms and moving into action again, this time more quickly. The last of her belongings packed, and Emmaline's money safely tucked into a sewn-in pocket inside her dress, she was ready to wake Reggie and snag the first mail coach she could find, to whatever town it was headed next.

It did not matter where she went next, did it? Any small town would do to start over. Her future looked bleak no matter what backdrop she chose. It would be a life lived simply and without hopes of a dashing earl who'd offer for her hand.

Small price to pay, really.

This cozy safe haven, the school, the earl, Miss Grayson and the other girls...she'd always known she would have to leave them behind. This life had never been for her, and she knew it. She told herself that as she carried a fussing Reggie down to the great hall and through the drawing room where she'd had her first kiss.

A kiss that had turned her world on its head.

All part of a fairytale life that had never been hers, not if she wanted the anonymity that would keep Reggie safe.

She just wished her heart would listen to reason.

She blamed that heavenly kiss for her distraction. Passing through the scene of the crime, as it were, she let her mind wander back to that moment, reliving every detail so it would be burned into her memory to be replayed over and over until the end of her days.

"I will admit, you are slightly more clever than I'd expected." Duncan's voice behind her made her freeze. Her limbs went numb as shock, and fear collided in her belly, making her feel sick and winded at once.

The house was quiet but for his voice, which was so level,

so calm. Like they'd bumped into one another in Kensington Garden and not in this dark, nearly deserted townhouse late at night.

She spun around to face him and wished she hadn't. He was close. Too close. And now Reggie was between them. Addie's grip on him tightened, and he made a sound of protest, still half asleep and unaware of the danger that surrounded him.

Duncan's smile made her bones turn to ice as he made a tsking sound like he was berating a small child. "What a naughty little girl," he said. "What were you thinking, running away from Uncle Duncan like that?"

She took a step backward but froze again when his smile faltered. The glimmer in his eye went from jovial to cruel and back again so quickly she thought she might have imagined it. Months ago, she might have chalked it up to imagination. She *had* done just that multiple times, telling herself it was merely her imagination.

But now she knew better.

He hid it well behind his easy smile and his quick laughter, but this man was rotten to the core.

Rotten and insane.

He gave her small, cajoling smile that didn't fool her one bit. Holding his hands out beseechingly, he took a small step forward. "Come now, Addie. Be a good girl and hand over the boy."

"I'd die first," she bit out between teeth clenched with fear.

He tilted his head to the side. "I was truly hoping it would not come to that."

"You have lost your mind," she hissed.

"No, my dear, I'm afraid you are, addled one." He spoke so evenly, so pleasantly. That alone was chilling. "After all, everyone knows that you were already beside yourself with grief after the loss of your parents. To lose your brother, too?" He tsked again. "Why, it would be too much for any young girl to handle."

Panic raced through her, curdling the contents of her stomach and making her feet feel leaden as some distant part of her brain scrambled to form a plan. To run or to scream for help? Screaming would only bring the housekeeper, maybe the old butler if he heard. They were no match for a young, strapping man like Duncan. "Why?" she managed.

He looked puzzled. Amused, even. "Why? Why what?" There it was. A flicker of insanity that made her certain of her next move. She had to get out of this house. Run as fast as she could and scream her head off as she did.

Someone had to be around. It was London, after all. Even in the dead of night, people were around.

"Why, why, why?" He repeated the question dazedly as he gave her a look of confusion. "Why, what, my dear? Why would I want to be the lord and master of my own estate?" he asked. "Why would I want to have enough money to pay off all my debts?"

"If it's money you want—"

"It's money I need," he shouted, losing all pretense at civility. "I owe debts to people far crueler than I," he said, his voice softening again as he shifted closer. "They do not forgive debts, and they do not allow anyone to walk away."

"Fine, then, if it's money you need—"

"You asked me 'why,'" he interrupted. "Well, I have a question for you? Why should a little brat like *him* get all the riches when he's done nothing to earn it? What makes him so special?"

"My father—"

"*My father, my father*," he mocked her in a high-pitched voice. "I am tired of hearing about your precious father. Would you like to hear about *my* father? He was your relative, you know. Your father's cousin, but he came from the bad side of the family, you see." He sneered and took a lunging step forward that made her scream as she turned her body to better protect Reggie.

"No one will believe you," she said. "I'll tell them—"

"You'll tell them what? That your kindhearted, generous guardian gave you a fright? It would be my word versus that of a young grief-stricken girl who few people have even met before. I'll take my chances."

"I won't let you do this!"

He laughed, and that laughter was worse than any shout or curse she could imagine. It skittered over her spine and made her knees grow weak with fear. "You say that as if you had a choice."

He lunged before she could turn and flee. She managed to crouch to the floor, using her body to shield Reggie, her scream for help turning to a shriek of pain as his fingers dug into her hair, and he wrenched. His other hand clawed at her face, her neck. Her screams turned to whimpers as she did her best to protect Reggie, who wriggled and wailed within her tight embrace.

Duncan's voice turned to an indecipherable growl as he clawed at her, muttering curses with a frenzy that made her think he'd gone over a ledge that he'd never come back from. "You stupid girl," he started. "When I get my hands on you—"

He broke off with a shout as Addie felt him torn off her. Cool air replaced the weight of Duncan's hands on her body, and she slumped to the side, gasping in relief as Reggie wailed beside her.

"You bloody son of a—" The rest of the growl was lost in the sound of punches and strikes as a fight broke out beside her.

Tolston. She recognized his voice at once, but the sight of him there, red with anger, his hair tousled in the melee. He looked too good to be real.

For a moment she had to wonder if she'd survived the altercation with Duncan at all. Maybe she had died, and this was heaven.

He looked like an angel to her now, all avenging right-eousness as he battled her enemy. She gasped and held Reggie tighter as Duncan landed a blow that sent Tolston staggering backwards into an end table. But rather than come for her, Duncan fled toward the front door shouting something about retribution and payback as he went.

The sudden silence when he left was stunning and brief. "Are you all right?" Tolston asked, stumbling toward her with a franticness about him that made her chest hurt. His hands were moving over her face, her shoulders, her hair as she assured him she wasn't seriously hurt. He did the same to a still-crying Reggie before bolting toward the door, following in Duncan's wake.

The housekeeper burst into the hallway with a fire iron overheard making Addie's heart leap with fear before she recognized who it was wielding the weapon. "We're okay," she said, though her shaky, breathless voice said otherwise. Scooping up Reggie, she shoved him into the housekeeper's arms. "Watch him, I must help Tolston."

CHAPTER 12

Alec always thought true murderous rage would cloud a man's vision, but this was not the case. In fact, he felt more clearheaded than ever before. His priorities were indisputable.

Keep Addie and her brother safe.

Kill anyone who tried to harm her.

Addie was safe. Now it was time to wreak vengeance on her attacker, whoever that man was. He paused for only a heartbeat outside the front door, his breath coming in ragged gasps, his hands clenched at his sides. Then he heard the sound of a horse's whinny around the corner, and he bolted in that direction.

There he was. Stumbling haphazardly and clutching at his ribs with one hand as he snatched for the reins of the horse he'd hitched nearby for a quick getaway.

What had he been planning? To kidnap Addie? Her brother? Both of them?

Questions would have to wait. Keep her safe, kill the man who harmed her. Rage had him barreling toward the other man, who turned at the last second and lunged toward him.

Knife.

He became aware of the flash of silver at the same time it pierced his side. A glancing blow before Alec struck his arm away, the knife flying out of his hand as he tackled him to the wet ground.

Rain made their wrestling bout a slick mess as mud had them scrambling, their limbs and hands scrabbling for purchase as they tried to best each other.

Thunder had the horse whinnying beside them, rearing up in distress at the sounds and the scuffle.

A shout from the road had him looking over, and the sight of Addie running toward him—toward danger—had him acting on instinct. *Go to her, keep her safe.*

The attacker might get away, but he had to make sure she was safe from harm. He'd gone no more than a foot in her direction when chaos broke out in the form of thunder, lightning, and Addie's shriek.

He saw her eyes widen in shock, but she wasn't looking at him, she was staring behind him. He spun around and watched as the horse reared up on its hind legs again, its eyes rolling with distress as it kicked and reared, heedless of the still body beneath its feet.

The attacker had been trampled.

A few moments later, Alec had managed to steady the horse and pulled the man from further danger, but it seemed as though the damage had been done.

"What can I do, my lord?" The old butler, wrapped in a robe, appeared at his side, staring down at the prostrate man with the feeble pulse.

"Call for the doctor," Alec said, though a large part of him wanted to say *let him rot* and walk away.

Between the two of them, they got him back into the house and laid him on the couch. Miss Grayson and the others hadn't returned yet, and once the doctor arrived and the servants were busy assisting him, it was only Alec and Addie left, waiting quietly by the fire.

"Is Reggie all right?" he asked, breaking the silence as he handed her a glass of spirits, that she stared into as if it was a mystery, but she did not take a sip.

She nodded. "He will be. I got him back to sleep." Her lips curved up in a humorless smile as she turned her glance from the liquid in her glass to him. "Can you imagine? He's back to sleep as if nothing ever happened."

He sank onto the settee beside her, noting the way her hands clenched the glass in her hands and a shiver had her trembling despite the heat of the fire. Wrapping an arm around her shoulders, he nudged the glass with his free hand. "Take a sip, it will warm you."

She looked at the glass but didn't lift it to her lips. "I—I do not feel *anything*. Is that normal?"

He squeezed her shoulders, his heart aching in his chest for this woman who had been through so much. "You will. I'd wager you are in shock at the moment. Your body and mind are processing all that has happened."

She nodded. "I suppose you are right."

"We'll have the doctor look at you when he's done in there with..." His voice faded as he realized he still had no idea who that man was.

"Duncan."

He stared at her, willing her to share. Not wanting to push her, not like this, but needing her to trust him.

She turned to him with a trembling lower lip, and he forgot all about his pride, his hurt feelings over her lack of trust. "Hush, little one," he said, pulling her closer until she rested against his chest. "There will be time to talk later."

She nodded against his chest, and for a moment they sat in silence, the only sound the crackling of the fire and a distant sound of servants bustling about, doors opening and closing. They sat in silence for so long, he'd begun to think she'd fallen asleep. But her soft whisper cut through the silence. "Thank you."

He squeezed her shoulders. "No need to thank me, love. Haven't you learnt yet that there is nothing I would not do to keep you safe?"

She turned slightly, burying her face in his chest and clutching at his jacket so fiercely that the cloth crumpled in her fist. At last she wept, and he held her close as she let out all the fear, the anger, the relief.

Stroking her hair, he held her tightly, wishing he could do more but not knowing how. He found himself murmuring reassurances into her hair. Telling her it would all be all right, that she and Reggie were safe now. That nothing bad would ever harm them again.

He wanted it to be the truth. He wished he could keep that promise, but the truth hovered in the back of his mind.

She was not his to protect. Maybe she never had been.

She was not his—not yet.

But she would be.

At least, he hoped she would be.

It was only now though that he fully understood how little he knew of her, of her life. And *that* he vowed to remedy.

When she was ready.

The arrival of Miss Grayson and the other girls put an abrupt end to their intimate moment. The doors flew open, and the normally cool, calm, refined Miss Grayson looked more flustered than he'd ever seen her. "What is going on here?"

Addie bolted upright, startled and embarrassed, no doubt.

"I-I'm sorry," she started, before he cut her off by pulling her back into his arms. Propriety be damned. He shot Miss Grayson a meaningful look. "I will explain all later, but first..." He nodded down toward Addie. "She needs rest."

Miss Grayson recovered herself, turning toward the handful of girls who were staring wide-eyed at the scene before them. "Prudence, tell Mrs. Baker we will need a hot bath. Delilah, Louisa, help Addie to her room, won't you?"

The lively redhead and a dark-haired beauty rushed forward, wrapping their arms around Addie and helping her to her feet, and leading her slowly toward the door.

She paused, looking over her shoulder at him, her look oddly pleading.

"Go," he said, mustering a small smile as weariness and exhaustion dragged at his limbs. "Go and rest. We shall speak in the morning."

She hesitated briefly but gave him a little nod of understanding before allowing the other girls to lead her away in a huddle of comforting murmurs and concerned whispers.

Once she was gone, it was just Miss Grayson who looked down at him, hands on hips as she considered him. "You look awful."

He ran a hand over his face. "It has been a long night."

She sat beside him. "Want to tell me about it?"

A weary sigh escape as he turned to her. "I can tell you what I know, but I'm afraid we'll both have to wait to hear the full story until Addie has had some rest."

Miss Grayson's brow was creased in concern. "Poor dear has been through quite an ordeal."

He grunted in agreement. "I'm starting to think we don't know the half of it." In the quiet of the night, he related what he did know of Addie's tale—starting with the fact that Reggie is her brother and ending with the attacker's injuries from the horse.

He'd barely finished speaking when the somber doctor came in to inform them that his patient had not survived.

Miss Grayson went over to the doctor, and Alec was dimly aware of their voices—Miss Grayson's soft with compassion and sadness for a man she'd never met.

Alec supposed a better person than he would mourn the loss of another, but at the moment all he could think of was the sight of that man's hands on Addie, of the crazed expression on his face as he'd attacked the woman Alec loved.

Love. There was that word again. He supposed he suffered from some form of insanity as well, falling for a woman he knew so little about. But if there had been any doubt before, there was none now—not after he'd nearly lost her.

Never in his life would he forget the all-encompassing fear that had gripped him at the sight of Addie in danger. Never would he forget the sensation, the knowledge—instant and impermeable—that this woman was his other half. His soulmate. All the things he'd once believed to be the things of myths and fairy tales.

When the doctor left, Miss Grayson came back over to him with a sigh. "He's making arrangements to move the body. There's nothing more to be done tonight."

He nodded, a new weariness settling over him as the first rays of dawn began to fill the room.

"Come," Miss Grayson said as she led the way toward the hallway. "We have an extra room made up for visitors. You can sleep there for the night."

He nodded. Sleep. That was what he needed. In the morning he'd see Addie, and maybe then he'd get some answers.

CHAPTER 13

The morning sun woke Addie, and for a moment she forgot all that had happened. For one brief moment, she forgot where she was and why. And then it came back in a rush.

She sat up with a start. "Reggie!"

"He's fine, dear." Miss Grayson was on the other side of her room, opening the curtains and arranging the contents of a tray. "We let you sleep in." She glanced over her shoulder with a kind smile. "It seemed as though you might need some rest."

She nodded as she fidgeted with the edge of her covers. "Thank you."

"Louisa is playing with Reggie in the library," she said. "And Lord Tolston is waiting for you downstairs in the breakfast room..." She turned back again, a whole new sympathy in her eyes as she added, "Whenever you are ready."

Addie pressed her lips together as a surge of emotions rose up in her. Did Miss Grayson know? Did she suspect? Was it written all over her face that she'd gone and fallen in love with her rescuer?

Or maybe the other woman just assumed, because, honestly—how could she *not* fall in love with a man as good and kind and honorable as Lord Tolston?

She supposed it was inevitable.

Belatedly, Addie realized there was one person Miss Grayson hadn't mentioned, and the mere thought of him had her sitting up straighter, rigid with apprehension. "What about Duncan?"

Miss Grayson's brow furrowed in confusion for only a brief moment. "Duncan. That was the man who attacked you?"

Addie nodded.

Miss Grayson came forward and sat on the edge of the bed. "I don't know who he was to you, and I hope this does not cause you too much pain..."

Addie found herself holding her breath as she waited for Miss Grayson to finish.

The other woman laid a hand on hers. "I'm afraid he passed away last night," she said. "There was nothing more the doctor could do."

Addie waited for...what? Relief? Sadness? Regret? She wasn't entirely sure what she was supposed to feel, and maybe it was that jumble of inexplicably intertwined emotions that had her eyes tearing up all over again.

The threat was gone. Reggie was safe.

A man was dead.

She could not be happy about the news, but she couldn't help but feel relief, either.

Miss Grayson squeezed her hand. "Are you all right?"

She nodded, swiping at her eyes. Stupid tears. How tired she was of weeping. "I am," she said. Then she added, "I will be."

"You know, Addie..." Miss Grayson took a deep breath as she seemed to search for words. "None of us know what you've been through, but I just want you to know that you will always have a home here at this school, for as long as you need. I have no doubt Lady Charmian would agree."

Addie couldn't speak. She was too busy blinking away tears again, but this time they were tears of joy. Her heart swelled with gratitude for all the beauty that had come from such a terrible situation.

And she owed so much of it to Tolston. Without him, she would never have found Miss Grayson or Louisa and the other girls. She would not have found a home where she could be with Reggie.

She would not have experienced love.

She only hoped now that it wasn't too late. She'd run away from him; she'd kept so many secrets; she'd lied to him.

Would he still want her now after all she'd done? After all *he'd* done?

She nibbled on her lower lip as confusion warred with relief and a million other emotions.

A knock on the door had her turning with a quick inhale.

Was it Alec?

Miss Grayson seemed to sense her alarm. "It's likely Louisa and Delilah," she said gently. "You gave those girls quite a fright last night." Her expression turned wry. "You gave us all a fright, but I suspect you experienced more terror than the lot of us combined, so don't let them bully you into talking."

She let out a huff of laughter, the sensation oddly familiar and unfamiliar all at once. With the threat that had been hanging over her no longer looming, she almost felt like herself again. But also, entirely new. She'd grown up these past few months—she'd learned what she was capable of and discovered just how brave she could be.

She thought back to the way she'd run from Tolston.

She'd also learned how vulnerable she could be. How weak in the face of overwhelming emotions.

She shoved aside the duvet. Not anymore. It was time to start a new day. There was no use hiding secrets, not anymore. Miss Grayson and the other girls deserved to know the truth, and no one deserved it more than Tolston.

When the knock sounded again, Addie called out for them to come in.

Sure enough, it was Delilah and Louisa at her door, with a smiling Reggie in her arms. "May we come in?" Louisa asked.

Delilah was already halfway across the room. Prudence showed up behind Louisa, peering in.

"Come on in," Addie called out. "All of you."

Miss Grayson left as they entered, giving her visitors a reminder not to pester her with questions until she was dressed and fed.

"Why didn't you tell us you were some well-to-do lady on the run from a dastardly villain?" Louisa exclaimed the moment the door shut behind Miss Grayson.

Prudence tsked like a schoolteacher. "You read too many gothic novels, Louisa."

Louisa ignored her, eyes wide with excitement. "Did that man really come to kidnap Reggie?"

Addie drew in a deep breath, ready to start with her explanations, when relief came from the unlikeliest place.

"Leave her be," Delilah said. "Can you not see she's been through a nightmare? Let her have some tea first before you bombard Miss Hopewell with questions."

Addie jerked back a bit at the sound of her name. Her *real* name. "You know who I am?"

Delilah's smirk was smug. "I figured it out." With arched brows, she gave a haughty sniff in the face of the other girls' gaping. "What? I keep my ears open, and last night there was talk about how the Hopewell girl ran off after her parents died." Silence fell, and Delilah shifted uncomfortably as she glanced over at Addie. "Sorry," she said, her voice quiet.

"That's all right," Addie said. "It's true. They both passed away, and that man who attacked me last night was our guardian."

Delilah held a hand up as Louisa opened her mouth to ask more questions. "Let's not make her tell her tale more than once, shall we?"

Louisa looked like she might argue, but Prudence stepped in. "Delilah's right. It's bad enough she lived through this ordeal, and she'll be telling this sordid story soon enough when she goes downstairs to see Lord Tolston."

They all eyed her oddly at that, and her cheeks burned. How much had they heard about Tolston's involvement?

How much could they figure from the blush in her cheeks at the mere mention of his name?

Against all odds, her silly mind was replaying his proposal. Of all the things to be thinking about at a time like this. She gave her head a little shake as she accepted a gown that Prudence had brought in with her. "It might be too big, but we can lace if tight in the back."

"Thank you," she said. Her gaze turned from Prudence, who was smiling gently, to Louisa, who looked like she might burst if she couldn't ask more questions, to Delilah, who was busy pouring her a cup of tea from the tray that had been brought in. "Thank you," she said again. "For everything. I know that my being here has done nothing but hurt the school's reputation, and yours as well, and I—"

"Oh please," Delilah interrupted with an unladylike snort that seemed so very uncharacteristic coming from the elegant, spoiled debutante.

Addie gaped at her as Prudence added, "Delilah is right. You have nothing to apologize for."

Now she turned her shocked stare to Prudence, who seemed to live up to her virtuous name.

Louisa grinned. "I think what they're trying to say is—if we've ended up here, we likely don't have much of a reputation to ruin."

"But—" Addie started.

"I think what Louisa's trying to say is...this school might have been started for fine young ladies," Delilah said. "But everyone you've met was sent here because their families didn't know what else to do with them."

"Precisely," Louisa said. With a mischievous grin, she added, "You aren't the only one with a scandal."

Prudence sniffed. "Speak for yourselves. My family has nothing to hide."

Delilah let out a laugh. "No, perhaps not. You, like me, were merely in the way. They didn't know what to do with *you* any more than my family knew what to do with me."

Prudence scowled, but she gave a little shrug of defeat. "Fine. Perhaps you both are right. We here at the School of Charm are all a bit wayward, I fear."

"But," Addie started again, her gaze seeking out Delilah, who'd pointed out more than once how bad her being here was for the school's reputation. "You've said many times—"

"And I was right, no doubt," Delilah interrupted. "But the truth is, we all have our faults and our problems." She looked to Addie. "Though I dare say none are quite as dramatic as yours."

Louisa sat beside her on the bed. "What I think Delilah means is that, though your situation might have been the most dramatic, you'll not find a better place to be than here amongst friends."

Addie heaved a heavy sigh. "Friends," she repeated. "I haven't had many of those before."

"I've never had any." Delilah surprised them all with that

little outburst, and her cheeks turned pink when the others turned to stare at her.

"Well, now you both have a whole house full," Louisa said with a cheerful grin that included both Delilah and Addie. "You'd better get used to it."

"Come along," Prudence said, her tone prim and impatient as she reached for the gown. "Let's get her ready. Poor thing has to face the Earl this morning. Gossip can wait."

The mere mention of Tolston had butterflies swarming in Addie's stomach. She had no idea what to expect, or how he would look at her.

She had no idea what to say.

When at last she was ready, she nodded to her new friends, feigning more confidence than she felt. "Let us not keep him waiting any longer."

Just outside the doors to the drawing room, Louisa placed a hand on her arm. "Do you want us to stay out here?"

She bit her lip. What she wanted was a moment alone with Tolston, but with Miss Grayson already there, it wouldn't happen. "Come in," she said. "I'd rather not relate the story twice so I might as well get this over with."

Delilah threw open the door, and Tolston rose to his feet. Stoic as ever, his expression was impossible to read. But his eyes...his eyes spoke to her just as clearly as they had the first time she'd seen him.

Concern, relief, affection—it was all there. But there was a wariness about him now, too, as he waited for her to speak.

"Thank you, Lord Tolston," she said as she took the seat he offered her. "Thank you for...for everything."

He gave her that lopsided smile she'd grown to love so much. "I am just happy you are all right."

His gaze met hers and held. There was so much she wanted to say, but this was hardly the time nor the place. Drawing in a deep breath, she turned her focus to Miss

Grayson and the other girls and started from the beginning. "My real name is Miss Adelaide Hopewell, my father was the Baron of Wrencliff..."

By the time she was done, the room was silent except for Reggie's occasional babble as he played with a piece of string Louisa had provided.

"That..." Louisa said slowly, her voice filled with awe. "That was even more dramatic than my novels."

"Louisa," Miss Grayson murmured. "Would you please take Reggie to the kitchen. See if you can find him a treat, would you?"

"Of course." Louisa seemed to come back to her senses, and the other girls followed suit. They filed out of the room, casting her looks of sympathy and support as they went.

When it was just the three of them, Miss Grayson gave her a warm smile. "I'll just be over here catching up on some correspondence should you need me."

And just like that...they were alone.

Well, alone but for Miss Grayson, but she was on the far side of the room with her back turned.

For the first time since she'd sat, she forced her gaze in his direction. She hadn't been able to meet his eyes until that moment.

"You have been through quite the ordeal," he said.

She bit her lip, sadness sweeping over her at the way he was looking at her. Like she was different now, or at least like he saw her differently. There was a new formality between them—which was only right, she supposed. She was no longer his maid, his charge, his damsel in distress, and she was afraid to think he no longer even thought of her as a friend.

She was merely a young, unmarried lady who'd lied to him from the moment they'd first met.

"Why didn't you tell me?" he asked.

She opened her mouth and shut it again. She had no good answer.

"Did you not trust me?"

Oh, her heart ached at the hurt she saw in those warm brown eyes.

She shrugged helplessly as she searched for the right words. "I did not know you."

He met her gaze evenly as he nodded his understanding. "It seems I did not know you either."

She wasn't certain he'd meant for the words to sting, but she felt as though a sword had lanced her chest. She held her breath until the sharp pain passed. "I did not know who I could trust," she said. "I feared no one would believe me."

He nodded. "I understand."

She bit the inside of her lip as the silence stretched between them. They'd never experienced awkward silence before—but then again, they'd never been together like this before either. Her sitting there as a proper young lady, him the notoriously eligible earl...

"I am sorry you didn't feel you could trust me," he finally said.

She wanted to say something to make this right, but words failed her. "I had to make sure Reggie was safe," she said. "That was my only concern."

"I understand."

She thought he might say more, address the fact that he'd proposed to her less than twenty-four hours before, but instead he shifted to face her better, his tone less familiar and his expression all that was proper. "So, what now then?"

She blinked in confusion.

"Will you stay here?" he asked. "Or would you prefer to find relatives to take you in? Perhaps you'd like to be escorted back to your home."

She thought he must not know how much it hurt to hear

him talk like this. Like she was a stranger. Despite all odds, they'd formed an intimacy these past weeks. A friendship, even. It may have been strange and irregular, but it had also been genuine and true.

To hear him speaking like this—polite and forced—it hurt more than she could bear.

Any hopes she might have harbored that this thing between them might survive, withered inside her. She'd done nothing but lie to this man. A man who'd done nothing but help her.

What had she expected?

What had she hoped?

That he'd still wish to marry her? That he'd forgive her lies, ignore her lack of trust, and tell her that he loved her above all others?

Tears stung the back of her eyes, but she would not cry. She bit the inside of her cheek to keep the tears at bay. She'd made her choices, and she would live with them. She would not beg this man to give her a second chance.

He eyed her oddly when she did not immediately answer. "Addie? If you wished to return to your home—"

"No," she said quickly. "I—That is, not yet." The idea of going back there alone, with only Reggie to keep her comfort in a house filled with memories, both good and evil…it was too much to think about.

"Very well." He nodded slowly. "It would be my honor to assist you however you wish to proceed."

"You have already been too kind," she managed. The thought of him helping her to move on…without him. She sucked in a deep breath. "I will go to the Havershams," she said, deciding it as the words came out. "Lord Haversham was a relative of my father's. He will no doubt know what to do about Reggie's guardianship and the estate."

Something seemed to shut down in Tolston's expression.

Where once she'd been able to read him, he was now a hard slate. Not unkind, just unreadable. Like he was no longer allowing her access to his inner thoughts.

She tried to ignore the coldness stealing over her. "I truly appreciate all you have done for me, Lord Tol—"

"Alec, please," he interrupted. With a small, rueful smile, he added, "After all we have been through, I hope to call you a friend, and wish for you to do the same."

She nodded, forcing a smile of her own. "I should like that."

It was a lie, of course. The last one she'd tell this man, she promised herself. It would be rude to deny his friendship after he'd saved her life and Reggie's. And yet, she did not want him for a friend. As a friend he would be a bitter reminder to all she'd come so close to having, all she'd run away from.

She could not expect him to propose again, not after she'd run like a fool.

"Alec, I—"

"Addie, I—"

They started and stopped at once, sharing a small smile at the awkward exchange.

"Ladies first," he said.

She swallowed. "I just wanted to say again how much I appreciated your assistance. I should have trusted you with the truth from the beginning, and I am sorry that I did not."

He studied her for so long she began to grow uneasy.

"You were right," he finally said. "You did not know me well enough to trust me. After the betrayal of trust you'd gone through, how could you know you could trust me?"

It was true, and yet her heart fought against it. She *should* have known. She *had* known. She'd just been too scared to admit it. Not just for her life and Reggie's, but for what that would mean. She'd been afraid to let this man any closer or give him any more power over her head and heart.

She'd been afraid to fall in love.

So silly, really, when she'd gone and fallen for the man anyway. And now it seemed her foolish fears had kept her from having him in the end. "Thank you for understanding." It came out as little more than a whisper, and she hated the formal way that he stood and said his goodbyes.

Wait, don't go.

But he was gone. Out the door before she had a chance to make things right.

CHAPTER 14

A
mazing how much could change in a fortnight.

"You look lovely, Addie." Emmaline smiled at Addie's reflection in the mirror.

True to his word, Tolston had helped to put everything to rights. Like the ever-dutiful Earl that he was, he handled the investigations, he dealt with the solicitor who held the financial power over Addie and Reggie, and he'd even been the one to tell Lord and Lady Haveresham the full story of what had transpired.

They believed him, of course.

They might have believed her, too, if she had trusted them with the truth from the beginning. But there was no use second guessing her every decision—that was what Louisa kept telling her.

Despite the Haversham's offer to house her and Reggie, she'd talked at length with Miss Grayson and Lady Charmian, and had decided for the time being at least, that she and Reggie would stay put.

She'd finally found a place that felt like home, and she

hated the idea of uprooting Reggie once again. He loved it at the school and so did she.

But even being content there hadn't changed the fact that she missed Tolston.

Desperately.

"Do you suppose he will be here tonight?" Emmaline asked the question that had been burning in Addie's brain ever since Lady Haversham had announced that they would be throwing a party in her honor at their home.

She'd been spending her afternoons with the Havershams, along with Reggie, and the kind lady and her husband had suggested that a party announcing her debut into society would be the best way to squash any rumors or gossip that had been swirling ever since the night of the masquerade.

Emmaline sat beside Addie at the vanity, which they were sharing to prepare for tonight's grand ball.

"Who?" Addie said.

Emmaline laughed, taking a hair pin out of her hands. "Do not play dumb, dear. It does not suit you."

Addie sighed. Of course she knew to whom Emmaline referred. There was only one gentleman who they'd discussed in great detail these past two weeks, and only one man who was forever on her mind.

Tolston.

She hated the way he'd left. Hated even more that she hadn't seen him since.

He's a busy man, that was what Miss Grayson kept saying, her expression kind and understanding and filled with just a hint of sympathy. Addie suspected Miss Grayson was well aware of her feelings for Tolston, but neither of them acknowledged it aloud.

But Miss Grayson was correct. Tolston was a busy man to begin with, Addie was sure, and his schedule had been that much busier dealing with the aftermath of her drama.

But busy or not, she could not help but think that he was avoiding her. And could she blame him? They'd grown intimate too quickly, their rare friendship forming during her darkest days.

Whatever connection they'd forged had been fierce and frantic. Maybe it had been too intense—a brief, powerful flame that flickered and extinguished rather than a slow simmering burn that could last a lifetime.

"Mother invited him, you know," Emmaline added.

"Did she?" Addie knew she had. The older woman had mentioned it several times, while searching for some sort of reaction.

Addie had no idea what Lady Haversham had heard or how much Emmaline knew, but she was determined not to fuel her own hope, and the last thing she needed was their optimism. That would only make it harder to move on. To move *forward*.

She would find someone new, that was all. This was the start of a new day. A brand-new chapter in her life.

By the time the ball started and she paused at the top of the staircase, waiting to be announced, she'd almost convinced herself that she was not disappointed he would not be there to dance with her.

Almost.

While she'd gotten somewhat used to lying to others, lying to herself had never been Addie's strong suit.

When the first strains of the next song began, she started her descent, focusing all her energy on keeping a smile on her face as she scanned the crowd for Louisa's red hair, Emmaline's tall frame, or Delilah's inky black coif.

She could use a friend by her side tonight as she answered what were sure to be a host of questions from curious members of the *ton* who'd caught wind of the gossip that swirled around her.

Halfway down the steps, her footing stumbled, and she clung to the rail as a lady with impossibly high hair shifted and she saw him.

Tolston.

He was here, and he was watching her with a gaze made of fire. She could feel the heat of it as his eyes moved over her, taking in the fitted gown and the upswept hair.

Friends. They were friends, she reminded herself. That was why he was here.

And yet...there was nothing friendly at all about the way he was looking at her.

When she reached the bottom, she let herself be swept away by the crowd of interested society members—some who were familiar, and others who were introduced to her right then and there.

But nothing could distract her for long from Tolston. She could feel his eyes on her no matter who she was talking to. No matter which way she walked in the room, he was always nearby.

It wasn't until partygoers started to enter the dining hall, and the room began to clear a bit, that he approached.

"Addie," he said softly. "You look beautiful."

"Alec." His name came out on a breath, and she realized too late that she had nothing else to say. Emmaline, who'd been at her side, slipped away without a word, and they were alone.

Well, they were alone in a crowded room.

"How are you adjusting back to life as Miss Adelaide Hopewell?" A hint of a smile played over his lips, and she remembered viscerally what those lips felt like pressed against hers.

Friends. They were just friends now.

She gave her head a little shake. "We are doing well," she

said slowly. "Reggie is doing well—he's found his best friend in Louisa, I believe."

He smiled at her attempt at a jest. "And you?"

"I—" She almost lied. *I am well.* She couldn't manage it. "I am adjusting," she said. "I think I am still figuring out who I am now."

He watched her so raptly, paid such close attention, like every word she said mattered. It was unnerving, but also rather lovely. Spectacular really. No one had ever made her feel more important, or so very cherished. That look had more words spilling out of her mouth, happy to confide in the man she'd grown to trust so well. "I do not feel like the same girl I was when I fled my home," she said. "But I am not certain I know who I am to be in this new life, either."

He nodded. "That makes sense. You have been through more upheaval than most experience in a lifetime. Give yourself time."

"Time, yes, of course."

"I'm sorry I've been gone for so long," he said.

She widened her eyes in surprise. "There is no need to apologize to me," she said. *I am no longer your problem.*

"But there is," he said. "When I left you last..." He glanced around suddenly as though worried he'd be overheard. "I ought to have explained my intentions."

She furrowed her brow in confusion. "Your intentions?"

"You did not trust me with your secrets." He said it boldly, baldly—the words hanging between them like an accusation.

At least, that was how she heard it.

Blinking wildly, she fought this panicky feeling she'd been harboring all day—all week. For a fortnight to be precise.

It was the horrible feeling of regret. Like she'd ruined everything that was good between them, and it was too late to go back and fix it. "Please, Alec, I can explain."

"No, Addie." He cut her off, taking her gloved hands in his.

She caught her breath at the touch. His voice was achingly gentle as he continued. "That is what I wanted to explain to you," he said. "There is no need to explain yourself. There never was."

She blinked up at him in confusion, and then her breath left her in a whoosh because he didn't even try to hide the emotions there in his eyes. Longing, regret, sadness, hope...

Love.

The earth seemed to shift around her, the rest of the party fading into nothing as the world came down to this man, this moment.

"When I left, I knew that you were right," he said, his voice little more than a growl. "You'd said you did not know if you could trust me because you did not *know* me, and you were right."

She opened her mouth to protest, but he shook his head. He wanted to finish.

He deserved to finish.

She clamped her mouth shut, her heart racing in her chest.

"After hearing your story, it became clear that I didn't know you all that well, either," he said. "And yet, I felt like I did."

She blinked, emotions choking her throat, but she forced out the words. "I felt the same."

She was rewarded with a slight hitch of his lips as he squeezed her hands. "We had a connection, my love, an understanding."

Her lungs stopped functioning when he called her *my love*. The words echoed through her skull and made her heart leap with joy.

Love. *This was love.*

"We had a connection that I will never be able to explain as long as I live," he said with a soft smile. "But I rushed things. I didn't give you a chance to get to know me, or me you," he said. "That wasn't fair to either of us."

She licked her lips. "W-what are you saying?"

He let out a huff of air. "I knew what I had to do. I needed to give you space to settle into this new life. Sort out your emotions."

She shook her head. Was that why he'd avoided her this past fortnight?

"That is why I focused on making things right for you...as much as I could," he said. "I want you to have options. Whether you want to return to your home or stay at the school, you and Reggie ought to have every choice. I don't want you to make any decisions based on...." He cleared his throat. "Obligations."

"Decisions?" She narrowed her eyes. "What decisions?"

He leaned forward slowly. "The next time I ask you to be my bride I want you to make that choice freely and clearly, without feeling that you are indebted to me because I helped you when you needed assistance."

The breath rushed from her lungs, and her head was spinning.

"Are you all right?" he asked.

Happiness. Pure, unencumbered joy that she'd never felt before made her heart feel like it might burst out of her chest.

"I must tell you, Miss Addie Adelaide..." His voice was a murmur as amusement stole over his features. "While I enjoyed our first encounter immensely, I would prefer not to have you fall at my feet again."

She blinked once. Twice. "Do you mean it?"

He grinned, and she saw her happiness reflected there in

his eyes. "That I do not wish for you to swoon? Undoubtedly."

She let out a shocked laugh. "No, I meant... Do you really wish to marry me?"

"One day," he said, tugging on her hands until she stumbled closer. Too close for propriety sake, but then again—he'd just asked her to be his bride.

Well, not in so many words. "Did you just propose to me?" she asked, all the wonder in the world in her voice.

His grin turned roguish. "Not exactly."

She sighed, but even his teasing words could not make her smile fade. "Alec, are you toying with me?"

He shook his head. "Never. It is just that I want to be clear about what is happening here. You were right before. You did not know me well enough to place your life in my hands—"

"And yet," she interrupted. "I *did* place my life in your hands, and you saved it quite admirably."

His smile warmed her from head to toe. "Miss Addie Adelaide, I mean to court you. I intend to give you all of the romance and courtship we skipped over in our short period of time together."

"You *do* know that is not my name, do you not?"

He merely grinned at her, love in his eyes and a roguish tilt to his lips. "Let me court you."

She tilted her head to the side. "Does that mean you rescind your proposal?"

"Never. It merely means I don't wish to hear your answer until the end of the season. At that point, if you deem me worthy to be your husband, I will happily make you my bride."

She couldn't help but laugh at that. "Me? Deem you worthy? Must I remind you, up until recently I was your maid."

He tugged her even closer, ignoring everyone around them. "You were never just that, not from the moment I met you. I've never known anyone like you, Addie, and I never want to lose you."

She rested a palm to his chest, feeling his heart thump in a strong steady pace beneath her hand. "I may not have trusted you with all my secrets, but that spoke more to my own fears than to my faith in you." She drew in a deep breath and met that warm, loving gaze she so adored. "I think I trusted you from the very moment I met you. Some part of me fell in love with you from the very start."

His eyes grew soft and tender. "Ah love, are you saying what I think you're saying?"

She smiled through her tears of joy. "Yes, Lord Tolston, I will allow you to court me."

EPILOGUE

 *ne year later...*

"ARE YOU CERTAIN YOU ARE READY FOR THIS?" TOLSTON asked.

Addie smiled up at her husband. "I have you by my side, do I not? Together we can face anything."

He smiled down at her, dropping a kiss on the top of her head as she rested against his shoulder. It was in the early stages yet, but if all went well, by this time next year, they'd be traveling with a babe of their own, as well as Reggie.

Luckily Reggie had been sleeping for most of this trip north. They'd need him cheerful and rested for the home-coming that was ahead.

"This is his home," she said softly, not wanting to disturb Reggie.

"His home is with us," Tolston said, his voice gentle as he laced her fingers with his.

"Yes, but this is his to inherit," she said. "Along with the title and the wealth. It's good that he come back often." She was saying it more for herself than anyone else's benefit. It was not that she did not want to make this trip—she just knew that it would bring with it so many memories and emotions that had been laid to rest.

But she knew she could not avoid her past—the good and the bad—for any longer. She and Tolston were starting a future, and it was time to reconcile with the past. Besides, Reggie ought to know this place. One day it would be his to control.

Until that time, Tolston had taken over guardianship and financial power for the boy. Between Tolston and Addie, they'd put the estate back in order—hiring on the servants who Duncan had let go and making sure that everyone in the area knew what had really happened.

They turned a corner, and the far edges of the country estate came into view.

Addie found herself holding her breath, but whether it was from fear or excitement, she could not say. Perhaps a bit of both.

"Well?" Tolston said when the estate came into view.

She smiled. "It's exactly as I remember it."

He shifted so he could wrap his arm around her and hold her tight. Always her hero, even in the quiet moments when all she needed was a strong shoulder to lean on and a listening ear.

It never ceased to amaze her all the ways he'd become her support and she his.

During a long and delightful courtship that spanned some six months, they learned one another's likes and dislikes, their habits and their backgrounds, their pet peeves and their foibles.

And through it all, they fell ever more in love.

They'd married in an intimate ceremony that had involved Reggie and her friends from the school of charm, and Addie had never felt more confident about the path in front of them.

Coming back here felt like the end of a chapter, one that marked the start of a new adventure.

"After this trip, I suspect it will all be over," she said.

"How do you mean?"

She looked up to see him gazing at her with that now-familiar, but still powerful warmth. The tenderness that spoke more than words could say.

She drew in a deep breath as she tried to put it into words. "I'm ready to put all that happened last year behind us," she said. "I'm ready to let go of the anger and the fear." She pressed into him. "I'm ready to start fresh with you, and Reggie, and this baby."

He nuzzled the top of her head, and when he spoke, she heard the regret in his voice. "I'm just sorry that you were forced to leave your home the way you were." He sighed. "I know it all worked out in the end, but when I think of what might have happened—"

"But it didn't," she interrupted. Tilting her head up once more, she gave him a light kiss that had him pulled her against him even tighter.

"I might have left here under unfortunate circumstances, but I cannot be sorry for all the changes it wrought." She smiled and saw his lips tug upward as well. "It brought me to you."

Now it was his turn to kiss her—and his kiss was far less brief and much more thorough. When he pulled back, she was breathless and dizzy with delight.

"Just think," she said, glancing over at her home that was getting ever closer. "If I hadn't left here, I never would have found you and fallen in love. I never would have made such incredible friends..." She drew in a deep breath and let it out slowly. "I might never have discovered a strength in myself I hadn't known was there."

Tolston squeezed her shoulders. "You were always strong. You would have realized that without Duncan's help."

She grinned. "Maybe." She flattened her palm over her belly. "But the fact still remains—if the bad events had not occurred, I might never have had all that I have with you."

He gave a huff of irritation. "Let us not think on that, shall we? It's too distressing."

She laughed, because she knew he was teasing...but only partially.

Her gaze roamed over the familiar fields, the trees she'd used to climb, and the stream where she used to swim. "I was a child when I left this place," she said. "I was innocent and naïve and believed in things like fairy tales and happily ever afters."

He kissed the top of her head again as he murmured, "And then you grew up."

"Exactly." She smiled up at him. "Now I *know* that some fairy tales do come true. And sometimes, if we're very lucky, we get our happily ever after."

He laughed. "Well then, Miss Addie Adelaide. I suppose you and I are very lucky, indeed."

ABOUT THE AUTHOR

MAGGIE DALLEN IS the author of more than a hundred romantic comedies in a range of genres including young adult, historical, and contemporary. An unapologetic addict of all things romance, she loves to connect with fellow avid readers. Come say hello on Facebook or Instagram!

.

Printed in Great Britain
by Amazon

27145800R00099